UNTOLD TALES

SPARK OF CHAOS: PREQUEL

SABRINA FLYNN

Published by Ink & Sea Publishing

www.sabrinaflynn.com

ISBN 978-1-955207-18-8

ebook ISBN 978-1-955207-19-5

Prequel of Spark of Chaos

Cover art by Mon Macairap

*To Justin
you were right*

fell wastes
Northolt
NÜThaaN
Isle of wise ones
le'eNtas
kambe
drack
whitemount
wyrim's fist
iile

Truth and lies are the warp and weft of legend.
—*Minnow, Sage of Mearcentia*

ALSO BY SABRINA FLYNN

Ravenwood Mysteries

From the Ashes

A Bitter Draught

Record of Blood

Conspiracy of Silence

The Devil's Teeth

Uncharted Waters

Where Cowards Tread

Beyond the Pale

A Grim Telling

Spark of Chaos

Flame of Ruin

God of Ash

Untold Tales: Prequel

Bedlam

Windwalker

www.sabrinaflynn.com

EYE OF THE STORM

Frostmarch, 1992 A.S. (After the Shattering)

THE SOLDIER ADJUSTED his fur mantle, tugging loose the top-most lace to let the air find his skin. Virgin powder sparkled beneath the noon sun. The sky was clear and pine filled his senses, sharp with cold, and fresh with life. For now.

Farin Thatcher eyed the circling scavengers in the sky, like a whirlwind of black marking death. He nudged his mount in the vultures' direction and his men followed in his mare's path, moving steadily towards the gorge.

It went without saying that whatever was rotting wouldn't be inside the gods' forsaken Scar. But Farin hoped it wasn't on the edge. He didn't like the endless tear in the earth, or for that matter, heights, especially with the recent wave of earthquakes. Unfortunately, there were too many birds for a deer corpse, and he couldn't call himself a scout of the Empire if he didn't investigate.

He signaled his scouting party to dismount, ordered one man to guard the horses, and strapped the wide snow nets on his boots. The soldiers fanned out, approaching the area like a net of their own—alert for bandits. Travelers were common enough in Northolt—even this time of year—and supply caravans had been constant for the past twelve years. With the Fell invasion at an end, it'd be a shame for a wayward caravan to fall into the hands of bandits. Supplies were scarce, and so were people.

The soldiers closed in on the area below the circling birds, moving swiftly over the snow, crunching with every step in the muffled quiet. Their path took them ever closer to the gorge. Much to Farin's dismay, the eye of the storm lay at the edge. He signaled a hasty halt, and crouched behind a tree to gaze at the split in the earth. Snow and ice and trees flowed right up to the sudden drop, as if the earth simply given up, and collapsed.

The vultures were screeching above, circling, but not landing. How odd. Farin signaled for his men to wait, and crept forward in the snow, from trunk to trunk, towards the queasy edge and a great tree that had clung there for millennium.

Farin Thatcher froze. The ancient tree was half dead. White patches mottled its wide trunk, spiraling upwards, as if it was fighting its demise. Some branches were bare, while others were full and thriving. Farin recognized the tree. A week ago, the magnificent pine had been as healthy as ever, standing the test of many harsh winters.

Farin had never seen such a thing. His gaze travelled to its base, where the roots wrapped around the edge of the gorge. The tangle of thriving bark and dying white battled here, too. His heart skipped, and he tensed. A woman stood in the tangle of roots and snow—she was naked.

The scout narrowed his eyes. The woman's hair was the flare of autumn leaves, and her skin was touched by the sun. She faced the tree, nearly hugging it, exposing a spine that flowed into a delicious backside. He thought of a summer peach, and his mouth began to water. Farin's body was confused: all at once, heat rushed to his loins, and a shiver ran up his spine. He edged closer, cautious but eager, unable to take his eyes off the woman as he rounded the next tree trunk. His new spot afforded a better view. There was a mark on her back, a tattoo of a sprawling oak.

The soldier followed the woman's curves to her ankles, and his eyes widened with fear. Her feet were roots and her arms were *inside* the trunk.

The startled soldier nearly pissed his pants. A witch —on his watch. Farin cursed his luck. As the witch stood facing the tree, a blackness crept over the earth between roots that were slowly turning white. She had put some kind of curse on the tree. And he did not know what to do.

He signaled sharply at his men to ready themselves. They rushed forward, not silently, but not loudly either. Still, the witch did not turn. He had never seen a Blight hag before, but he had heard plenty, and he feared to find what the beautiful witch's face would look like—probably warty, or worse, a man's face. But with that backside—Farin shook the thought from his mind and focused on his task, or tried to at any rate.

When his men were in position, each as wide-eyed as he, Farin burst from behind his cover, arrow notched, prepared to draw his bow. "In the name of Emperor Soataen Jaal, stand back from the tree, Witch."

The witch did not move, did not acknowledge his presence. Farin shifted on his feet in the snow, and cleared his throat, trying again. "Stand back and surrender!"

Still, no movement, not even a tilt of her head. The soldiers looked to their sergeant. Taking a deep breath, Farin edged forward, poised to draw and fire. With every footstep, he saw the blackness spread over the ground like ink, surrounding the tree and seeping from the earth. The vultures were directly over the gorge, circling, but not diving towards its darkness. Rot assailed his nostrils and he nearly gagged.

The stench was unbearable. He dared not take a step closer. Farin raised his bow, drew back the string, and let loose his arrow. It hit the target, a knot in the trunk, directly in front of the witch. The twang snapped her from the ritual. She jerked in surprise and took a step back, hands returning to those of a normal woman. The roots released her legs. She staggered back on bare feet, dazed and shivering in the snow.

From there, everything went horribly wrong.

The ancient pine quivered, its bark bulged, as if something living sought exit from its innards. The pine turned white and began to bleed. Inky backness seeped from its lifeless bark, running rivulets down its length. Its needles fell like ash, and where they touched, the ground turned black.

The witch scrambled back as the snow melted. Something writhed beneath the soil, wiggling, moving, the ground was no longer solid. A soldier screamed. Farin glanced towards the sound. One of his men was caught in the earth, blackness crawling up his flesh, swarming over him and dragging him down.

"Run!" Farin yelled. He staggered back from an inky patch as the witch climbed to her own feet. He found himself running with her, away from the pulsing tree. Her face was not warty, or that of a man's, but as beautiful as the rest of her body. Her eyes were like leaves, and they held the essence of spring, and fury.

She quickened her pace, running for the forest.

"Stop!"

The witch did not stop. Farin lunged, reaching with his bow, catching her ankle between string and wood. She tripped, slamming hard onto the earth. She twisted, opening her mouth, but before she could speak, Farin clubbed her over the head, silencing whatever ritual she was about to unleash. The witch went still. However, the earth did not.

Desperate, Farin hoisted the witch over a shoulder, and bolted after his men as the earth heaved, rising like a wave.

Farin Thatcher ran, and he did not look back.

2
THE WISE ONES

Wintertide, 1993 A.S.

OENGHUS SAEVALDR SHIFTED on the ridge. The foliage cracked under his weight and the branches overhead creaked with cold. In response to the frigid landscape, the kilted berserker's tender bits wisely shriveled up for protection.

"What do you make of it?" a deep voice whispered in his ear.

"Never seen anything like it." His eyes were bright in the chill, focused on the valley below: the barren basin and the castle-crowned hill. The land between the ridge, from valley to castle, was black and waxy like a frostbitten limb. Twisted trees reached from the earth like white bones from flesh.

"It's not Blight, then?"

"Don't know," he answered.

The distant castle appeared untroubled—its walls were intact at any rate.

The dark man at his side cursed under his breath.

Oenghus glanced at Captain Gaborn Oakstone. "I've seen a lot in my time, but I'm not all knowing."

"It was the 'Wise One' part that gave me hope."

"Well, aye, the wise part tells me to walk in the opposite direction of—that." Whatever *that* was.

"And we'll walk right into the headsman's axe when we tell the Field Marshal we turned tail," Gaborn pointed out.

Oenghus snorted. "I'll fight an army, but this is better suited for—"

"Someone with brains," the stout woman on his other side finished.

"Or a death wish," Oenghus mumbled.

"I, for one, am tired of lying on this frozen ground." Morigan Freyr climbed to her feet, smoothed her skirts, and checked that her tightly coiled hair was in order. Oenghus had a sudden urge to unpin his companion's hair. When Morigan let her hair down, she plowed like a razor beast in heat. He stood to hide his reverie and reluctantly pulled his thoughts towards the rotted earth.

Brains, he reminded himself, the Emperor needed brains. Then why the Void had the Field Marshal of Kambe sent Oenghus Saevaldr to scout the pass?

Morigan marched down the ridge towards the waxy blackness. He caught up to the stout healer in a few quick strides, and placed a large hand over the shorter woman's shoulder. She turned a dark glare on the giant.

"Hold up, Mori" he hissed. "At least let me go first."

Morigan glanced at the watching soldiers gathered

on the ridge. "We certainly can't spoil your reputation, now can we?"

Oenghus scowled at the healer. Hoisting his shield and hammer, he strode down the hill with Morigan on his heels. Both Wise Ones stopped at the end of the slope, standing ten paces back from the black earth.

"It's creeping," Morigan observed, "like ice along a window pane."

Slowly, but steadily, the rot was spreading. But Oenghus wasn't sure if it was rot or ice or even oil. He sniffed the air. Sharpness pricked his throat from the chill.

Morigan lifted her skirts and moved cautiously forward, right up to the line. She cracked a frozen branch from a tree and extended the tip towards the border of unknown.

The tip pierced the earth. "It feels like a bog—or decay." She withdrew the tip, but the waxy ground clung to the stick like strands of a spider's web.

"I don't like this," Oenghus grumbled, stepping beside her. He scowled at the expanse and the distant castle. His hand flexed around the handle of his war hammer. He preferred an enemy he could bash, not one that ate the earth.

Morigan leaned towards the tip of the stick, squinting at the substance. She summoned the Lore, a low murmur that flowed from her lips. With her free hand she wove a ward against disease, and then traced a complicated pattern over the tip of the stick.

Runes swirled to life, encasing the blackness. The enchantment throbbed, the weave expanded, pulsing once before stiffening. The runes turned hard in the air and shattered like ice.

Morigan straightened in shock. A trickle of blood seeped from her nose.

"You all right?" Concern cracked the barbarian's facade.

"Well enough. A slight backlash." She dabbed at her nose with a handkerchief, and shook herself, letting the stick fall into the unnatural ground. The stick moved, first one end, and then the next, until the tip disappeared beneath the surface. The trio watched with growing unease as the ground swallowed it.

Morigan shook herself from the trance. "It's not Bloodmagic. It's not Blight—"

"Void," Oenghus cursed.

"I think so," Morigan agreed. "We should get help."

"You two *are* the help," Oakstone reminded the Nuthaanian woman. But just the same, the captain fingered his bow nervously, itching for a target of flesh and blood, of a land with trees and rivers.

"I'm not much help with this sort of thing," Oenghus admitted.

The blackness spread another foot, and Morigan took a hasty step back. "I'm not either. I can heal people —not the land, but at this rate, it'll reach the next stronghold in a week."

Oenghus scanned the countryside, taking stock of the valley. This tip of land was a spike from Kambe that had driven a wedge into Nuthaan before the two empires had made peace. Northolt was aptly named. It stood guard over the borders of the Fell Wastes, Nuthaan, and Le'Entas, at the edge of Kambe's northern most border.

"It may have already spread into Nuthaan," Morigan added softly.

"Right, then." Oenghus shouldered his targe and gripped his war hammer with both hands.

"Oen—" Morigan's warning fell on deaf ears.

Oenghus summoned the Lore with a thunderous chant that shook the valley. Blue energy crackled to life around the weapon and he brought it down, slamming steel and power into the ground. The waxy shell cracked with a spray of sludge. A jagged line rippled from the hammer's head, ripping the earth apart, lancing the wound to reveal the rot beneath.

"Oh, dear," Morigan huffed.

A thick mass of black maggot-like creatures writhed beneath the earth, bodies bulging with their feast. These were no ordinary maggots, unless the flies that had laid them had been as large as eagles.

Oenghus wrinkled his nose. He glanced down at his boots and quickly shook one of the creatures loose. It fell into healthy soil, and burrowed beneath the earth. Blackness began to spread from the burrow like spilt ink on parchment.

"Some kind of Voidspawn," Gaborn spat the word from his tongue.

"Not Voidspawn, but tainted, I fear," Morigan sighed.

"So what's tainted these things?" asked Oenghus as if he fully expected her to know.

"It's our job to find out," Morigan said. She scanned the healthy earth, and moved over to a grouping of boulders. Oenghus stomped over to her, eyeing the snow covered rocks.

Long-time companions that they were, Oenghus sensed her line of thought. "The Void eats life, and so do maggots."

"After a fashion," she corrected. "And you claim you have no brains." Morigan pointed at a large stone and Oenghus obediently hooked his hammer on his belt and bent to lift the rock. He carried it to the edge of blackness and lobbed the stone onto the ground. It landed with a sickening squelch, but held.

"That's a lot of stepping stones, Morigan."

"You would," she sighed. Before Oenghus could formulate a retort, Morigan summoned the Lore, tracing an armor weave, layering stone over air and a loose bind. With a steadying breath, she stepped into the dead land.

Oenghus tensed, ready to drag her back to safety at a moment's notice, but her theory held, and so did the earth. The Void-tainted maggots ignored her presence. Healer, berserker, and captain let out a breath of relief.

"Can you manage the weave on the whole squad?" Gaborn asked.

Morigan glanced at the twelve waiting warriors. "I'll make do."

"Right before you die on your feet."

The stout Nuthaanian smiled at her towering kinsman. "The only way to die."

Oenghus grunted in agreement.

3
NORTHOLT

NIGHTFALL WAS NEVER far off in the north. The days were short and the sun never seemed to reach its goal, tiring and falling from the sky just shy of the heavens. A line of soldiers trudged through the bleakness, boots sticking to earth that was as black as tar.

The castle loomed closer, and Oenghus slowed, eyeing the open gates in the fading light. The castle on the hill had its arms open wide, but its battlements were empty and arrow loops dark. Unease prickled the back of Oenghus' neck. He stopped, and the line of soldiers followed suit.

Oenghus did not like standing out in the open, but there was nowhere else to go. As the captain and Morigan stopped at his side, Oenghus felt that the castle was made of eyes.

Gaborn was half crouched, arrow notched, itching for cover as much as the next soldier. "It looks deserted," he noted. The lean Kamberian's pointed ears were as sharp as his eyes.

"Abandoned," Morigan added.

"I'll send men to scout."

Oenghus stopped the captain with a heavy hand. "Nightfall is a tick away. No use wasting time."

"I suppose," the captain relented. "We'd all rather have stone at our backs when night falls than this rot."

No one voiced the words that lingered in their thoughts. Whether spawned or tainted, creatures touched by the Void thrived in the dark. Even if the scouting party had waited until first light to cross, the taint would have spread, making a crossing in full daylight impossible.

"Whatever happens, stay out of my reach, and someone keep a bloody eye on Morigan," Oenghus threw over his shoulder and received an answering snort.

Bones littered the road that wound up the hill. Skulls and femurs and knucklebones, all bleached beneath the chill sun, picked clean of flesh, spilling out of the gates and down the hill. Oenghus could sense the soldiers' unease behind him. Fear rippled against his back. Fear was good. It kept warriors sharp.

"It looks like they were fleeing," Morigan's hushed voice echoed in the emptiness as they passed a horse skull.

Oenghus tucked his shield in close, clenched his hammer, and marched through the gates. Stillness greeted him with a quiet shake. The courtyard and battlements were empty. More bones, more black earth, and—

"Look." Oenghus followed the captain's gesture. The inside surfaces of the walls and gates were scorched. "Check the gate tower," Gaborn ordered. Four of his men broke off from the group. They climbed the stairs to the battlements and disappeared inside.

"There," Morigan pointed, "on the temple." The temple was more fortress than holy place, but that was unsurprising, considering the bull's head adorning the front. Zemoch, Guardian of Justice, was a militant god.

"The crack?" Oenghus asked.

"Aye."

Oenghus and Morigan scanned the stone walls. There were more cracks in the stone—in the battlements and running along buildings.

"Poor upkeep?" Oenghus ventured.

"The earth has been shaking something fierce these past weeks," Gaborn said.

"Not uncommon this far north," Morigan noted.

A soldier appeared from the gate tower. "The oil's all gone, sir, but there's no bones up top. It's as if everyone abandoned the walls."

Oenghus scowled at the emptiness. "How long do we have on your weave, Mori?" he murmured to the woman at his side.

"The ward will fade with time and use. I don't honestly know," she admitted. Lines pulled at the corners of her eyes and lips. Multiple weavings had taken their toll.

Oenghus tugged on his beard and stalked to the center of the courtyard, planting his feet. He raised his hammer and slammed it against his targe. The echo thundered off stones. The Nuthaanian waited as he eyed the temple and keep, hoping that someone—something—would answer his bold challenge.

Morigan walked to the well and peered over the rim. When nothing answered his threat Oenghus huffed with disappointment, and joined her as she finished a light weave, dropping an orb into the well's center. It illuminated the stone.

"Empty," Oenghus said in surprise.

Gaborn joined the two. "It's fed by a natural spring, if I remember right. They built the well around it."

Oenghus tapped a jagged line on the well's side. "Wonder what else cracked." He eyed the ground, grunted, and stalked towards the main keep, deciding to start there. The doors were closed, but it appeared as if a saber cat had used the reinforced oak as a scratching post.

"Movement," the captain hissed, jerking his chin towards an arrow loop high on the keep. Oenghus leaned back. Whatever had moved wasn't there anymore. He tried the door. It was barred. Whether any human still lived inside was an entirely different matter.

Oenghus pounded his hammer against the reinforced wood. No one answered.

Gaborn stepped back and shouted into the fading light. "In the name of Emperor Soataen Jaal III, open this door!"

A scrape of bone answered.

Oenghus looked down. The bones were sinking into the earth. Horse heads, bones of cattle and dogs, and human remains—all jumbled together, picked clean of flesh and tendon. The bones disappeared.

"Bollocks." He slammed his hammer into the door again. "Open this bloody door or I'll crack it like an egg!"

The soldiers in the courtyard froze, fear creeping in with another movement of the earth. In a heartbeat, they bolted, rushing towards the battlements, seeking solid stone. Oenghus turned, putting his back to the door as the ground rolled. Gaborn notched an arrow. Voices rose from within the keep. Something heavy fell, metal rasped, and a smaller door opened in the larger.

"Hurry!" a frantic voice shot out of the portal. Oenghus shoved Morigan inside as the soldiers risked the earth, racing towards the keep.

The ground burst. Bones grabbed boots, raking flesh. A man went down and a creature of bone and maggots erupted from the black earth. Oenghus swung, shattering a scapula attached to a leg like a wing, but the amalgamation reformed. Black maggot-like creatures swarmed over the shattered bones, reshaping, repairing, and came up swinging. A horse skull, attached to a mash of bones that made up the spine of the snake-like shape, dove, piercing a soldier clean through.

Gaborn loosed an arrow. It bounced harmlessly off. His order cut through the chaos. "Inside!"

The bone snake lashed and rattled at the soldiers running for the door. Oenghus stepped towards it swinging, batting away its attacks with his shield, as he crushed and ground the bones to dust. But with every blow, it reformed. There was nothing Oenghus could do for the soldiers caught in its frenzy.

All at once, the snake dove beneath the earth. The ground rippled, moving towards the keep.

"We have to close it!" the fear in the voice was catching. Glancing over his shoulder, Oenghus moved backwards, grabbed Gaborn by the collar and shoved him towards the narrow opening. When Oenghus was the last man standing, he stepped back, hunching through the wicket. A soldier of the keep threw his weight against the door, closing it as others rushed to place the bar.

The entire gate shuddered as the bone snake threw itself at the wood. Soldiers rushed to shore up the doors, adding their weight while they dragged a heavy barricade into place.

Morigan tucked an errant strand of dark hair inside her bun, restored order to her skirts, and took stock of the men who surrounded her. They were a ragged bunch of warriors, all staring, stunned, fearing the Void-cursed creatures on the other side. The men turned their fear to something tangible, surrounding the new arrivals with weapons poised, prepared to push the newcomers out as a sacrifice if needed.

Oenghus took in the half-starved men. The castle guards' tabards were tattered and bloodstained, some of their eyes had the sheen of fever, and all of them were unkept. The door shuddered again.

"Positions!" one of the more confident men roared. "Light the oil. Shore up the second level." Half the weary soldiers rushed up winding stairs, relaying orders with echoing shouts, while the rest remained at the uneasy standoff.

"We're all Kamberians here. Where is your lord?" Gaborn asked with the tones of command. The captain had a face to match his voice, and his crisp blue and silver tunic of Kambe leant him an air of authority that was sorely lacking in the great hall. But rather than be reassured by his presence, the keep soldiers shifted. Their eyes darted from one to the other, and finally settled on the man who had shouted orders.

Oenghus did not like those looks, so he stepped forward, into the ring of steel, drawing their attention.

"I am Oenghus Saevaldr," he rumbled with a voice like thunder. "Wise One of the Isle, Bone Mender, Skull Crusher, the Bloody Berserker of Nuthaan and the Grimstorm of the Fell Wastes." With every word, the ring of steel retreated a step. "You may have heard of me." He swept his eyes over the remaining soldiers. "We have been fighting for twelve long years in the Fell Wastes, and want nothing more than to go home. I'll warn you, I'm already in a foul mood. So you best tell me quick what the Void is going on here?"

"A Portal to the Nine Halls."

"The Witch."

"The dead walk."

"The Void will swallow us!"

A tumult of voices rose above the noise of battle.

The man who had shouted orders, a bearded warrior whose face was streaked with soot, stepped forward. "We are stranded on this island of stone. How did you walk over the ground?"

The voices died. The constant scrape and thud of attackers beat at the soldiers' sanity.

Oenghus drew himself up to his full height, towering over their heads like a crag. "We took the stone with us," he grunted. Before anyone could ask how, he turned to the leader—a sergeant by his tattered insignia. "Your name?"

"Sergeant Farin Thatcher of Northolt. How did you bring the stone with you?"

Oenghus did not look at Morigan. He swept a baleful eye over Gaborn's scouts, warning them not to speak. Twelve had taxed her. A group such as this would destroy her like a ship of stranded sailors fleeing a sinking ship onto a raft. The raft would sink.

"Do you have injured?" Morigan asked, smiling at the weary group. "I'm a healer." Her motherly presence and kind tone were a balm to the soldiers' frayed nerves. They lowered their weapons.

"There are many," Farin answered.

"Our men will reinforce yours, Sergeant," Gaborn said. "How are your defenses?"

"The Swarm—it's what we call them—they attack all night, every night since the blackness spread."

A shout echoed from a higher level, cutting Farin's report short. Oenghus followed the rush of boots. The keep was under attack—that's all he needed to know.

Guards stood at every arrow loop, struggling against a flurry of bone supported by crawling black carrion. A pincher stabbed through a loop on the second floor, impaling a soldier. It wrenched the man off his feet and tried to drag him back through the space. He did not fit. Maggots dripped down the stark white bone, swarming over the victim. His comrades rushed forward with axes and torches, hacking and setting alight both victim and killer, burning one of their own in the process.

The soldier's screams echoed in the corridor and followed Oenghus towards a greater commotion. The door at the end of the hallway bulged. A cluster of men hurried to reinforce, but it was a losing battle, one Oenghus wagered they lost every night, being beaten back to the inner-most areas of the keep.

"We lose ground every night," Farin shouted, confirming his assessment. "There's no point defending the gates, the Spawn burrow underground and come up in the courtyard." In a lower voice, he added, "We're nearly out of oil."

As they followed Farin to the top most levels,

Captain Oakstone and his men broke off to contain a breach.

"We reclaim the keep during the day, but they keep coming—there is no end." Farin paused at a reinforced door, took a deep breath, and opened it.

Oenghus ducked under the lintel and stepped onto a high turret tower beneath the night sky. Stars shone like beacons, lighting horror beneath. The ground was alive, roiling in black waves, battering the keep with a relentless barrage of twisted bone.

The Void craved life, it thirsted for blood—for the life it lacked—twisting everything it touched.

"We need to find the heart," Morigan said at his side. "This is all just—fodder."

Oenghus gripped the crenellations, watching the struggle below. "Shock troops," he grunted in agreement.

Gaborn joined them a moment later. "When did the attacks begin?" he asked.

Farin Thatcher paled under the cold moonlight.

"Someone mentioned a witch," Morigan pressed. "Was it a Blight hag?"

Farin's lips remained pressed together. Oenghus began counting to ten; his patience gave out at five. He grabbed the soldier by the tunic collar and jerked him towards the battlements. "Speak or I'll find someone who will."

One look into the baleful gaze, and Farin broke. "There *is* a witch," he stuttered.

"What about her?" Oenghus growled.

"You're choking him, Oen," Morigan pointed out. Her calm voice brought him back. He glanced at the man dangling from his hand, mumbled an apology, and let Farin fall to the stone. He stood over the soldier and crossed his arms, waiting.

"We found a witch by the gorge. She was killing an ancient pine on the edge. Her... her hands," he hesitated, searching for his tongue, "Her hands were *inside* the tree and her feet were roots."

Oenghus frowned.

"The tree was half dead, nearly all white, and the ground between its roots was as black as it is here. She wouldn't listen. I loosed an arrow, just in front of her and she let go of the tree, but it was too late. The tree died, and the ground, it just... This happened. I pulled the witch along with me. We barely made it back to the keep."

"Is she still here?" Morigan asked.

"Yes." Farin confirmed.

"Where?"

Farin pointed over the wall.

As Oenghus turned to look, a shadow swept up and down, and he raised his shield, catching a pig's skull connected to a ladder of femurs on the wood. Black, wiggling carrion spewed from the skull's mouth, dropping onto the tower top.

Four bone pinchers stabbed into the group. Oenghus ripped the skull from its perch and bashed his shield against a stabbing limb, batting the attack away from the soldier on the ground. Farin scrambled to his feet, diving towards the door as some of the Swarm latched onto his legs.

Morigan leapt aside, the Lore on her lips. She tapped bone with a word. It cracked and shattered, sending maggots pouring onto the tower top.

"Hurry!" Farin cried at the door. Gaborn herded

Morigan through and Oenghus came barreling on their heels. The two men put their shoulders to the door and Morigan added her Nuthaanian strength, as Oenghus heaved the bar into place.

Farin screamed for reinforcements as he stumbled. He leaned against the wall for support, drew his knife, and pried at the clinging black creatures feasting on a gash in his leg.

The black maggots fell, sucking at the spattered blood on the stone. Oenghus removed his flask of Brimgrog, dipped a finger inside, and let a drop fall on each. The tainted shriveled up into black crisps.

Boots thudded in the hallway, and a squad of torch-wielding soldiers appeared. Oenghus hoisted Farin away from the battle, back down the stairs.

"The wound will fester; their touch taints," Farin breathed as if it would be his last. In a quiet corridor, Oenghus released the man, and Morigan bent to examine the lacerations on his legs. The carrion had eaten straight through cloth and skin—the tainted always had a voracious appetite.

"It kills flesh?" Morigan asked.

"Yes."

Morigan glanced at Oenghus who nodded at the look in her eye. The berserker put a hand on Farin's chest, pinning him to the ground, and held his leg still with the other.

"What are you doing?" The soldier struggled helplessly against the giant's strength.

"Healing you."

Morigan removed Oenghus' sacred flask from his wide belt, uncorked it, and poured Brimgrog over the man's wounds. Farin thrashed and strained and then went limp with defeat.

"Hurts like hornets on your bollocks, but they'll be no festering," Oenghus stated.

"Happen to you a lot, Oen?" Morigan raised both brows at her kinsman. He grunted, snatched the flask from her, and shoved the cork back in the top.

"Don't get your bun in a knot."

"Always your grandest wish. Now, then, let's meet this witch," Morigan said, wiping her hands on her skirts.

"Erm…" The soldier paled.

"Spit it out," Oenghus growled.

Farin licked his lips. "About the witch—there's a slight problem."

Oenghus narrowed his eyes. "*Where* is she?"

"The temple," Farin said, using the wall to hoist himself upright.

Gaborn, who had been watching the battle through an arrow loop, arched a brow. "You mean the one across the courtyard?"

"Aye."

Oenghus moved beside the scout captain and squinted through the narrow window.

The temple of Zemoch was a small fortress in its own right. Its stone had been chipped and carried down treacherous paths from the Fell mountains. Its windows were high, and its doors were made from solid Nuthaanian stonewood. One might as well take an axe to stone, as cut through that barricade. Save for a few, half-hearted attempts to breach its defenses, it appeared that the Swarm had left the temple alone.

Oenghus eyed the runes etched into the temple door. "And just why didn't you lot take refuge in the temple?"

"We got separated when the earth turned."

"But it's quiet during the day, you said. You're telling me you couldn't have fashioned a bridge of some sort?"

Farin scratched his scruffy beard, looking like an errant child. "They locked us out," he said quietly. There was shame in his eyes. "We wanted to kill the Witch, but the clerics—Inquisitor Ashe—disagreed."

Morigan frowned at the soldier. "You attacked the clerics, didn't you?"

"They struck first!" he defended. "The temple was split. Half wanted to burn her, and the others—well, there they are. If they'd only handed her over, we wouldn't be here." Lines of tension, near to breaking, leaked across his face. "I should have never brought her," he muttered.

"Bloody Void," Oenghus spat. As if they didn't have problems enough. They'd have to wait until sunrise.

4

THE WITCH

A CRACK OF sunlight broke the long night. With a rasp and rattle, the bone amalgamations collapsed, retreating into their waxy cocoon. The tainted took the dead, too. And the already-taxed soldiers rushed to put out fires.

Oenghus pulled Gaborn from the front lines, and together they sought out Morigan. She was in an over-crowded, makeshift infirmary—as she had been for much of the past twelve years. Dark shadows had taken up permanent residence under her eyes.

"And we thought we were done with this," Oenghus rumbled gently, handing her a waterskin. She drank gratefully and wiped her brow.

"Twelve years fighting the Wedamen—what's a few more days?" she shrugged.

He eyed her critically; a few days could be the differ-ence between survival and death. "The sun's up."

Morigan nodded in reply to his unvoiced question. She issued instructions to the healers, who had, before the attack, been cooks and chambermaids.

Oenghus led his group outside, onto the curtain wall. Men were scurrying on the walls, repairing and reinforcing defenses. Along the way, Oenghus found the scout captain. "Only us three." Glancing at Morigan, he wondered if she could manage that many weaves in her state.

The group filed down a stairway, and stopped on the steps, just above the black earth. It was a good fifteen feet to the temple steps. Oenghus could manage the leap, but not the others.

"I wonder if I could bind stone to the earth," Morigan mused. Oenghus twisted, looking up at the woman on the higher step. He wasn't keen on experimenting with a new weave—not yet anyway. Morigan, however, looked willing. She had that look she got whenever she was going to try a new remedy.

Before Morigan could summon the Lore, Oenghus walked back up the steps and planted his feet in front of a heavy stone crenellation that had been knocked from the battlements during the attack. He bent his knees, slapped his palms to the sides, and heaved. Lifting the stone, he waddled to the edge, and pushed the rock away from him. It fell, landing with a splat in the black earth, in the space between temple and stairway. The top poked conveniently out of the ground. Every soldier on the wall stopped to gawk at the feat of strength.

"Stone bound to earth," he grunted.

"Thank you, Oen," Morigan said. She lifted her blood-stained skirts and jumped from stair to stone to temple step. The others followed her lead.

Oenghus put his fist to the Nuthaanian stonewood as Gaborn shouted, "In the name of Emperor Soataen Jaal III, open this temple!"

There was no answer.

Oenghus pounded his fist against the door a second time. The entire temple seemed to shudder. He sensed watchful eyes staring from one of the stone Auroch heads glaring down at the group from high above.

"We're here to help," Morigan spoke directly to the statue's snout. Oenghus glanced back at the soldiers on the wall. Their eyes were desperate. How many clerics had they slaughtered in an attempt to kill the witch? Would the soldiers continue to try, now that an easy path was available?

The Void they would.

With a growl, Oenghus turned back to the impregnable door and threatened it with the weight of his hammer. "Open this door, or I will lay it to ruin!" This time, his bellow shook the stonewood.

A heavy bar was lifted on the other side of the door. The warding runes pulsed once and went dormant, fading back into the wood.

The door to the temple opened.

A thin, trembling man who was well into the Keening and dressed in dingy white robes squinted from the crack. His rheumy eyes confronted a banded leather breastplate and the folds of a kilt. The acolyte's neck creaked backwards, as he searched for the head on the towering figure.

Oenghus glowered down at the man.

"May we come in?" a pleasant voice inquired. Morigan elbowed her way past Oenghus, and smiled at the acolyte.

The man's shoulders slumped with relief. "Are you soldiers of the Emperor?"

"Captain Gaborn is," Morigan started to introduce

herself, but Oenghus had had enough pleasantries for one day. He planted his hand on the stonewood and pushed, hard. The door smacked into something that grunted. Just as he had suspected, the acolyte was bait.

Oenghus stormed in to find one dazed paladin holding a hand to his helm and two others with weapons drawn. He caught a sword on his targe and spun, putting the first paladin in front of his comrade.

"Oh, by the gods, put your weapons away." Morigan's sensibleness was louder than a shout. All four warriors froze like guilty children. "The Emperor has sent us to aid you."

Oenghus bared his teeth at the outright lie. Gaborn kept his mouth shut.

"Where's your priest, or Inquisitor, or whatever the bloody Void you call the torturer? Zemoch wouldn't let this bag o' bones scrub his chamber pot."

"Oen." Morigan elbowed the giant.

"How dare you speak of a Guardian in such a manner!" The square-jawed paladin who had been introduced to Oenghus' shield bristled.

A fourth paladin stepped from an alcove, dressed in blued-armor and Zemock's red and black tartan.

Oenghus eyed the large warrior. "Always hiding in your holes, frightening the weak to do your bidding."

Morigan looked at her kinsman, and sighed. But the tall, veteran paladin ignored the berserker, and looked to the more sensible of the two. "I am Knight Captain Keeling," he said, resting a hand on his sword hilt.

"Scout Captain Oakstone of the Emperor's Watch," Gaborn stepped forward with a salute. "This is Morigan Freyr and Oenghus Saevaldr, both Wise Ones of the Isle, both healers of renown."

The paladin rubbed his pale beard thoughtfully. "I have heard of you both." Whatever he had heard, it must have been one of the more favorable tales circulating about Oenghus, because the paladin seemed satisfied. "How did you traverse the earth?"

"We're Wise Ones," replied Oenghus, waving his fingers mystically at the man.

"How many men did you bring, Captain?"

"A squad to scout. Twelve men in all, but the army is waiting on the border of blackness."

"The men in the keep seem to think that a witch is responsible," Morigan nudged the conversation in the most pressing direction. "We wish to see her."

"The witch is the cause of all this—or so most think," Keeling explained. "The soldiers in the keep are screaming for her blood."

"Are you of a different opinion?" Morigan asked.

"No, but my superior is." His eyes darted towards a wide archway and a closed gate that revealed little of the inner sanctum. "I'll take you to the Inquisitor."

Keeling gestured, and turned towards the gates. With a brief prayer and a flare of light from his palm, the gate unlocked and he pushed it open, leading the way in, while his men barred the entrance behind them. The heavy gate closed on their heels, sealing them inside the grand hall.

Oenghus frowned at the stark waste of space and the towering rune-etched steel statue that dominated the opposite end. This far north, the Kamberians preferred Zemoch over Chaim or Zahra. Devotees of the Nuthaanian Guardian called him the Stalwart One. The statue's eyes were distant, facing north, ever watchful, ever ready to beat back the crazed

Wedamen. But it was the men who froze along the walls yearly who kept the hordes at bay—not the Guardian. Zemoch was nothing but a waste of good steel.

Oenghus eyed the giant flail that the Guardian held, the spiked ends dangling like merchant scales. Knight Captain Keeling raised a fist in salute as they passed. Oenghus, however, ignored the kilted Guardian. The group walked beneath a warded arch, down a long, equally stark hallway, and stopped in front of a reinforced door with a jailer's slat.

Keeling knocked. The slat was thrown aside. A pair of thoughtful green eyes looked through the peep hole, and a woman's voice demanded, "What is it, Captain?"

"Soldiers of the Emperor have arrived, along with two Wise Ones. They walked over the earth, Inquisitor." Keeling stepped aside, and the eyes narrowed as the paladin introduced the new arrivals to the Inquisitor behind the door.

"We're here to stop the taint," Captain Oakstone said. "We'd like to speak with this witch, Inquisitor Ashe."

"Step back," the Inquisitor ordered. "I'll allow Morigan Freyr to speak with—"

"Oh, by the goddess," Morigan rolled her eyes, "Stop with all the mystery and let us speak with your prisoner. You can either let Oenghus and me in, or we'll take our leave and let you all rot." She placed her hands on her hips, and Oenghus gulped. The gesture was never a good sign where Morigan was concerned.

A long moment passed as Ashe and Morigan locked eyes. Oenghus plotted who'd he'd knock out first before putting his impressive shoulder to the door. If needed, he was sure he could break the hinges right off the stone.

The Inquisitor's gaze flickered to Oenghus. "How old are you, Wise One?"

Oenghus scratched his beard, puzzled. He removed his hand from his unhelpful beard, and began counting the centuries off on his fingers.

"He's very nearly a thousand," Morigan answered.

"I have a good twenty years left," Oenghus growled.

"You Wise Ones may come. Step back and leave your weapons." With a sigh, Oenghus made a show of removing his war hammer, daggers and shield, and stepped back, passing the weapons to Gaborn. Morigan handed over her various knives and a sap that dangled from her belt.

A bar was lifted, the wards ebbed, and a latch was thrown. The door opened. A silver-haired, green-eyed woman stood in the frame, hand resting easily on a mace at her side. Farther down the hallway, a younger, black-haired woman in white robes stood with a cocked crossbow in hand. She looked nervous.

The Inquisitor stepped aside and jerked her chin at the Nuthaanians. Oenghus ducked beneath the lintel as he followed on Morigan's heels. The door slammed shut behind them, and a large helmeted paladin planted herself in front of the exit, sizing Oenghus up. He ignored the guard, jerking his chin towards the younger woman.

"Your acolyte best steady her finger."

"A precaution," Inquisitor Ashe explained. "We lost a good number of soldiers and civilians in the initial invasion, but most of them—they fought and killed each other."

"Over the witch?" Morigan asked.

"I'm not sure she's a witch," the woman admitted. "It's complicated." She turned on her heel and marched down a long hallway of tidy cells. Pristine stone and polished steel—the Blessed Order liked its walls white; it was easier to scour the walls, paint over the blood, and begin an interrogation with a tidy slate.

The back of Oenghus' neck itched with threat as he walked, fully aware that the young, twitchy woman with the crossbow was following at a deadly distance. The Inquisitor stopped at the last cell. Without his targe, Oenghus felt like a fish in a barrel—a target as large as he was hard to miss.

The Inquisitor turned to them both. "Sergeant Farin's report was very clear, and it was corroborated by the other soldiers who survived the trip back from the gorge. They all saw the same thing: a naked woman with her hands inside a dying tree and her feet connected to the roots. Ordinarily, this, coupled with the taint, would be condemnation enough; however…" the battle-hardened woman paused for a breath, "I think she may be a nymph. And if so, by the Law of our Order, she is the property of the Lord of the land, and I cannot simply execute the creature."

"Aye, the Law's always getting in the way of a good burning," Oenghus grumbled.

Ashe frowned at the barbarian. "You *cannot* deny this taint on the land."

"Why aren't you sure?" Morigan asked, distracting the two from each other's throats.

"I've never seen a nymph—only illustrations," Ashe admitted. "Have either of you?"

Oenghus tugged on his beard. "A handful of times."

"I have healed two nymphs in my lifetime," Morigan answered.

The Inquisitor looked relieved.

"Let's see her, then."

Ashe leveled a severe look on the hulking male. "I only let you in because of your age and race."

"That, and you had no other choice," Oenghus bared his teeth, and gestured at the door. "I promise I won't run off with your prisoner."

The Inquisitor unhooked a ring of keys from her belt, selected one, and inserted it into the lock. The door swung open.

A woman sat cross-legged in the middle of the cell floor, chained by a single shackle entrapping her ankle. Her hair was autumn, red as a changing leaf, and her eyes were spring, green as life eternal. Her skin glowed with summer, and the sight of the woman stole the barbarian's breath away, as sure as the chillest winter.

The prisoner wore a simple robe that failed to conceal her shapely curves. Oenghus eyed the sweep of her sharp ears. Definitely not Kamberian.

"Why is she chained?" Morigan asked.

"I thought it wise. There is no denying what the soldiers saw—she wields power that we do not understand."

"Fear," the woman said. Her voice was music, but it brought discord to the towering male. A wave of dizziness slammed into Oenghus. A torrent of memory, of soft words and eager lips, of love, burning like the sun in his breast. The eyes of spring stared at him with a knowing gleam.

Oenghus staggered backwards, transported. He was running. Every breath was agony and with every footfall he sank into a deep snow drift. A weight was slung over his shoulder, wrapped in fur, bumping against his back. The braying calls of a hungry pack beat between his ears and panted down his neck. A realm of ice stretched to the horizon.

He blinked, slapping his hand against reassuring stone: steady, solid, timeless and simple.

The Inquisitor stepped forward, shouldering past Morigan, and slammed the cell door shut on the prisoner. "She has bewitched him."

The trigger-happy acolyte raised her crossbow.

"Don't be absurd; he's a Nuthaanian." Morigan was at his side. "Oen?"

The man in question shook himself, and pushed off the wall, opening his eyes to Morigan's concern. "It's nothing," he said hoarsely. "Just thought I knew her. You know?"

The healer looked into the sapphire eyes of the ancient. She did not know, but being long-lived herself, she could guess at some of it.

"Battle fatigue," he grunted.

Morigan swallowed down a laugh. Grimstorm did not get fatigued. Instead, she turned to Ashe. "He'll be fine."

"Is she a nymph?" the Inquisitor asked.

"I would say so, but I'll need to examine her further."

"Until now, the prisoner has not uttered a word."

"Hasn't she?"

"No."

"Did you, or any of your men, lay a hand on her?"

"The Knight Captain was eager to interrogate her. However, the Law forbids us from interrogating a nymph. It would be as productive as questioning a dog."

"Right." Morigan smoothed her skirts. "Well, I've questioned dogs before, they're quite informative." The healer pushed the door back open, and this time, she stepped in before Ashe could stop her. Oenghus followed on Morigan's heels. Despite the Nuthaanians' towering presence, the woman on the floor did not appear to be frightened; instead, she looked worn.

"I'm Morigan Freyr. And this is Oenghus Saevaldr. Do you have a name?"

"I have many names," the nymph answered.

"Why do they fear you?" Morigan asked.

Green eyes flickered to the paladin. "She knows."

"You poisoned a tree and defiled the land," Ashe accused.

"Not I."

Oenghus moved between the paladin and the nymph, shielding her from her antagonist. "Are you hurt?"

"Yes."

Oenghus knelt. "Did the men touch you?" His question was a low growl.

"I am broken from the tree. I am weak."

Oenghus searched her eyes, trying to recall a name, a time, a when… anything at all. He felt as if he knew her, knew every strand of her hair, her every curve and breath. He was drawn to her, and could not bear to look away for fear she would vanish.

"We can heal you," Morigan offered.

"The land needs healing," the nymph said.

"Did you cause this rot?" Morigan asked.

"No."

"Were you keeping it at bay?" Oenghus questioned.

"No."

"Trying to stop it?" he tried again.

"Always."

"Always, what?" Ashe pressed.

"I arrived too late."

Ashe stiffened with impatience, but Morigan held up a calming hand, and voiced the question, "Too late for what?"

"An old wound has festered. I need your help." The nymph looked at Oenghus then, leaving no doubt as to whose help she required.

"Well," Oenghus tugged his beard, "who better to lance an infection than two healers, aye?"

The nymph smiled. And he remembered.

5

PASSION AND FIRE

An Unknown Age

SNOW. AN ENDLESS tundra of white and a dull orb that hung above the bleakness. The barbarian ran, his fur boots breaking the thin ice, sinking up to his knees in snow with every footstep. His breath swirled in the cold and his lungs burned. He had been running all night, with the relentless, hungry howls on his heels.

He lifted his leg again—another stride, one after the other, his heart pumping. What had started as an insignificant weight on his broad shoulder had become a crushing burden. The barbarian tightened his hand on the unconscious Goddess wrapped in fur, and cursed his impulsiveness.

A black spot entered the white—darker, bluer—an ice cave. Ulfhidhin glanced over his shoulder and made for it. The frost fiends were close, and there wasn't much time; they had followed his trail of blood.

The barbarian shivered from the elements, from exhaustion and fear. As he trudged up the slope to the cave, his beard rasped against his frozen furs. The cave gaped as he stood before it, gazing down its throat. A good place to make a stand, he thought as he took another step, and slipped.

Ulfhidhin wrapped his arms around the Goddess, shielding his prize as he slammed onto a sheet of ice. Momentum propelled him down the slope, into the cave. The barbarian's descent ended with a crack. Instinct propelled him to the side, rolling him away from a falling spike of ice. The frozen spear shattered on the floor, inches from his head.

He exhaled, resting his forehead on the warmth beneath his body. The Goddess moved beneath him, her eyes wide, struggling against the constricting fur and the weight of the wild-eyed man on top of her.

"Hold still," he growled. Sapphire eyes blazed. But the Sylph was not intimidated. With one final, jerking movement, she freed her hands and slapped her palms against her abductor's ears.

Ulfhidhin grunted, his ears rang, and he stumbled to his feet, shaking his head like an aggravated bear and nearly trampling the Goddess in the process. She scrambled away.

The barbarian unhooked his war hammer, retrieved his targe, and planted himself at the base of the ice slope. The first frost fiend, a bristling thing of crystalline shards, slipped down the slope, as surprised as the barbarian had been. Ulfhidhin swung his hammer, but the fiend recovered its footing and leapt to the side. He cursed, dodged a breath of burning cold, and swung again. This time the hammer connected with the fiend's spine, and it shattered into chunks of ice.

One down. A hundred to go.

Ulfhidhin faced the next, and the one after. His arms burned, and his lungs were heaving with effort as he fought exhaustion in the furious haze of battle.

When the dim sun retreated, Ulfhidhin still stood, surrounded by the frozen remains of his enemies. His shield dangled from his hand, dragging on the red snow. He could not find the strength to lift his hammer. The steel head rested in the shattered skull of its final victim.

Blood streaked the barbarian's body, pooling around his boots. He glanced over a shoulder, searching for his prisoner. She was gone.

"Bollocks," he grunted. With effort, he lifted his hammer an inch, and hooked it on his belt. His shield slipped from his numb fingers, and he staggered forward. He found her in the darkest corner, digging at the snow, clearing away the ice to expose the rock and hard earth underneath. The Sylph's skin glowed with luminous moonlight. But she was still flesh and blood; her entire body trembled and her fingers were raw. Despite the bite of cold, she splayed both hands on the frozen patch of earth, concentrating or perhaps, praying.

He snorted. To whom did a Goddess pray?

The sound snapped her out of the trance and she turned, eyes widening. A nasty bruise marred her forehead where he had hit her over the head the day before —or was it the day before that? He could not recall.

The Goddess of All, with hair of night and eyes like stars, drew herself up, clutching the heavy fur blanket to her body. "What do you want with me?"

"Want?" he asked. His voice was like gravel.

"You brought me here because you knew I was powerless, did you not?" Her silver eyes blazed. "At the very least, have the decency to introduce yourself before you plow me like a filthy beast."

The barbarian laughed, a sound that rumbled from his gut. "If you like," he shook the frost from his black beard and stepped closer—moving nearer with every word. "I am the lightning, I am the crag and the rocks and the raging storms. I am the sea and its roar."

The barbarian was close enough to touch her. And he did. He dared to grab the Sylph's hand and press her palm to his heart. She arched her neck, meeting his wild gaze, her breath quickened, and the air between them swirled with heat.

"I am passion and fire, and everything you cannot control." He let go of her hand, but her touch remained. Ulfhidhin pressed his palm against the cave wall, letting the ice burn into his calloused skin. "I want you safe," he said simply.

With his last morsel of strength, the wild god closed his eyes and willed the stone to obey. It heated at his command. When the rock glowed red, he slumped, and then slid, finally falling at the Sylph's feet.

6

AWAKENING

SHARED MEMORIES DWELT in two sets of eyes—a silent conversation between souls long intertwined. For a moment, Oenghus was that other man, and he wanted to reach out to touch her hand. But her eyes said *wait*.

Oenghus shook himself and stood, turning his back on beauty, facing the Inquisitor. "She's a nymph. They need sunlight, earth—life."

"Sunlight?" Ashe frowned. "I can't allow her outside, not with those soldiers, and as for life—that's precisely why we're stuck in here."

"What about potted plants?" Morigan ventured. "Surely someone in the temple or inside the keep grows herbs during the long winters."

The nervous acolyte shifted. "I do."

"Good," Oenghus nodded, and turned, crouching in front of the nymph. He touched the shackle around her ankle and muttered the Lore of Unlocking. It popped off and he tossed it away as if it were a serpent. The nymph sighed with relief as she rubbed her ankle.

"You can't do that." The paladins tensed, the crossbow came back up, and steel was drawn.

Moving very slowly, Oenghus turned his head to look at the three women over his shoulder. "And why not?"

"The nymph belongs to the Emperor. She cannot leave our custody."

"Your hospitality is lacking."

"Small wonder she did not want to speak with you," Morigan added. "Locking someone in irons is not conducive to aid. Let's worry about the taint on the land first, shall we?"

"Aye, you can worry about your finder's fee from the Emperor after," Oenghus said. Gently, he gripped the nymph's arm and helped her to her feet, but the brief touch was nearly too much. Another wave of disorientation hit the ancient. He swallowed it down, both wanting never to let her go and never to know anything of past lives lived. Frustrated, he left her to Morigan's care, and grunted at the acolyte to lead the way.

The hallway swayed as he walked in and out of memory, in the same body, the same eyes and skin—but different. Like an ancient mountain that had been slowly shaped and worn by time, he had changed.

Oenghus tugged on a braid and glanced back. The nymph was leaning heavily on Morigan. Had she bewitched him—planted these 'memories' in his mind? He shook unease loose. He needed to focus on the now. Not on his past, or any other's, for that is how he thought of the dimness beyond the veils, those lives as other men.

The acolyte, Katerina as she was called, kept a small greenhouse tucked in the topmost floor. Ritual stones heated it, and mirrors reflected sunlight from the two large Auroch statue eyes that decorated the edge of the temple. As soon as they entered, the nymph—he did not like to think of her by that other name—fell on the plants, sinking her hands into the soil under a small, potted lemon tree. She sighed. The leaves of the lemon tree grew and stretched as if they were being stroked by the sun itself.

Inquisitor Ashe and her guard watched, and slowly, Katerina lowered her crossbow.

"There's your proof," Oenghus grunted.

"Then she was helping the tree by the gorge?" Katerina asked.

"Trying to," Morigan replied. "Until she was interrupted."

"You said an old wound has festered, Nymph. How do we stop it?" Ashe pressed, but the nymph ignored the woman. Her eyes were closed—content. The Inquisitor stepped forward and grabbed the nymph's shoulder. "I asked a question."

Morigan placed a hand on Oenghus' arm, halting his rage before he intervened with lethal efficiency. "Inquisitor Ashe," she smiled, "nymphs are very much like deer. Startling them does not accomplish anything." With motherly briskness, Morigan brushed the paladin's hand off her charge and put her bulk between the two. "Your way has not been working very well so far, now has it?"

No one replied.

"Give the nymph some space." She shooed the Inquisitor back like a pesky hen. Oenghus was not surprised. He had watched Morigan do the same with the Field Marshal of Kambe.

"I will speak with the man," the nymph's soft voice entered the room.

All eyes turned to the source. When the Inquisitor had grabbed the nymph's shoulder, her robe had shifted, revealing the nape of her neck and the top of an intricate mark—the leaves of an oak. Oenghus' eyes lingered on that mark. He did not need to see the rest to know what it was, to know its shape, its leaves, the way its roots hugged her hips—he could feel the mark like a whispered touch on his own spine.

"Then speak to him, Nymph," Ashe gestured.

"Alone." The word hung heavily in the attic space. It felt as if the word had punched a hole in the floor and Oenghus would start falling at any moment.

"You won't leave my sight, Nymph."

The robe slipped a fraction, and the nymph shrugged a bare shoulder, returning to her tree.

Morigan glanced at Oenghus. He darted his eyes pointedly towards the Inquisitor and found a place to sit. The floor creaked in protest as the giant settled himself into the silence.

"Well," Morigan said, smoothing her skirts. "It appears we are at a standstill." Her tone left no doubt as to whom she blamed for this development.

"I cannot leave the nymph alone with a man," Ashe defended.

"I have known Oenghus for—far too long. And there is one thing I have learned about the *berserker*," she said, emphasizing the feared title. "He can be trusted to do what is right, and presently, Inquisitor, we need to get rid of this taint."

Ashe frowned in consideration. At length she warned, "Do not touch the nymph. Your word."

"Upon my honor, I will not lay a hand on the nymph." He touched his sacred Brimgrog, sealing his oath.

With a jerk of her head, Ashe ordered her women out and followed on their heels. Morigan directed a stern look at her kinsman before following.

The door shut.

"It's a good thing I'm a Sylph," the Goddess purred. Her eyes slid towards the Nuthaanian. He did not move. Memories were trying to find a comfortable place to settle in his mind. But the visions and sensations were a strange fit. "You look conflicted," she observed.

"Something like that."

"My poor love," she sighed. "You were always more comfortable with your manhood than your godhood." A mischievous spark in her eye reminded him of laughter. The memories settled. Oenghus stood and walked over to the Sylph. She rose with the grace of water and arched her neck to meet his gaze.

"Your eyes never change," she whispered.

"And you change like the seasons." With an unsteady hand, he touched her hair, brushing beauty.

"Do you like it?"

In answer, he grabbed her and brought her hard against his body. She was silk and power—it was like holding a waterfall. Oenghus wanted to merge with her and let her consume him. Her body responded to his, and warmth spread down his back, awakening the spirit that was forever intertwined with his. He cupped her face, staring into her eyes. "My heart."

"My earth," she breathed, savoring his heat.

"Why the Void are you here?" he growled.

"I need you."

"For this taint?"

The Sylph shook her head. "An unfortunate occurrence. I needed an ancient womb for this body. A younger tree could not support me. The old one was the closest to you, but the Void sensed my arrival."

"Does that mean every Reaper, Grawl, and Void-cursed madness will come sniffing after you now?"

"As long as I don't use my powers, Ul—Oenghus," she corrected. He was grateful that she had not used the ancient name of their first meeting. The Sylph could feel him, and she knew it might topple his sanity. "Not in a direct way at least," she continued. His hands fell to her shoulders. So warm and sumptuous, and so familiar. "If I used my power to clear this taint, then it would only make matters worse. As long as I am in this realm, I cannot raise a hand."

"Then why risk yourself?"

"I missed you."

"Bollocks," he snorted. "You could have come to me at night, as you sometimes do—in the disguise of dreams."

Full lips curved with delight. "I wondered if you knew."

"Knowing and admitting are two different things." Even now, the dormant bond was awakening on his back, his awareness of her growing by the moment.

She ran a hand up his chest, over his breastplate, toying with a braid in his black beard. "Your poor mind. Simplicity is what you crave. That's what I love about you."

"I thought it was my cock."

"The superior mind to be sure," she purred. All at once, the playfulness fled, and was replaced with a burden—a great weight that he felt pressing keenly on his own shoulders. With a sigh, she rested her forehead against his chest. Oenghus felt her weariness and despair as if it were his own.

"What do you need, Yasine?" he whispered her true name.

"Swear to me."

"You have my love."

"I need your obedience."

In reply, Oenghus brought his lips down hard and fierce over hers until the breath left her lungs. When the couple emerged for air, Oenghus growled, "I bow to no one—not even you."

"You've gotten on your knees frequently enough."

His mind went blank. And she hid a laugh against his neck. Somewhere during the kiss, her feet had left the ground, and he had no intention of putting her back.

"The Fate of countless realms depends on your obedience."

"I make my own Fate," he boasted.

"I need your seed."

Oenghus blinked. "Now?" His voice had gone very suddenly hoarse.

"So easily distracted."

"By you," he agreed.

"Any female. Frequently. Isn't that one of your Oath-bounds out there?"

"That was centuries ago—we have children," he added, feeling as if he were climbing a slope of very small pebbles. He set her back down. "It's not as if I see much of you."

"You never stay long."

Oenghus' head throbbed. "Don't bloody mention —" he cut off when he saw her smile. "You're teasing me, aren't you?"

"I've never tired of seeing you flustered, my love."

"That, and you're stalling for time."

"Time is the one thing we don't have," she sighed, glancing at the door, and then to his eyes. "I know you well. You are not a man who stands aside—no matter the name you bear."

"Never," he agreed.

"I need your courage, your will, your faithfulness." There was a haunted look in her eye, one that stilled his flippant reply about her growing list of demands. "This realm is lost, Oenghus. It is broken. What was done cannot be changed; what was broken cannot be mended —the fracture is too deep."

"Stop speaking in riddles."

"Trust me, my rock, *please*," she whispered like a brush of wings over his heart. "Support me, anchor me, be my strength—for once, I beg of you in the coming days, to stand still and do not react. Let them take me to the Emperor."

"I don't understand, Yasine. You sound like the Scarecrow."

"By the Light, I hope not, he is as broken and fractured as this realm." Mist clouded her eyes. "There must be a child, between you and me, and then let this body go. Let me die."

THE DOOR FLEW OPEN, slamming against the stone, nearly jarring the oak from its hinges. Oenghus Saevaldr ducked beneath the frame and glowered at the waiting women. The twitchy acolyte fingered her trigger, and the other paladins rested hands on weapons.

Morigan frowned.

Without a word, Oenghus stomped down the hall to the winding stairway, leaving the Sylph kneeling beside her thriving lemon tree. The swish of Morigan's skirts caught up with his long strides halfway down the stairwell.

"Oenghus?"

He did not stop.

Let me die. There had been something in her words— not the cycle of the Spirit River and the chance of rebirth—but something permanent.

An iron hand drew him up short with authority. "Oen," Morigan snapped, "if you do not tell me what is going on I am going to drop you to the floor." He stopped at the bottom of the stairwell. Oenghus blinked down at the healer, who looked about to make good on her word. "I'm beginning to worry that the nymph managed to put an enchantment on you. What *is* wrong?" Morigan whispered for his ears alone.

Footsteps were traveling down, towards them. There was not much time to explain.

Oenghus gripped her shoulder. "I know her, Mori."

"How?"

"It's ill luck to speak of such things." His hand tightened. "You know of my dreams."

Understanding sparked in her eye. "I see." And she did. One did not spend sixty years, on and off, as Oathbounds without knowing something of the other's nocturnal disturbances. "What now?"

"I am going to take care of the taint."

"She told you how to stop it?"

He ignored the question. "I need your best ward."

"Oenghus," she warned. "You're not going out there alone."

"I'll be fine."

"You need me to replenish the ward," she argued. The footsteps were nearing, and he turned, walking towards the exit with Morigan matching him stride for stride.

"You've been on your feet for a day and a night."

"So have you," she countered.

"I'm a berserker."

"And I'm a mother," she reminded. "Besides, you always make the worst decisions when you're angry, Oen."

He didn't have an argument for that. Morigan knew his bull-headed blunders well. He searched for a counter reply and snagged on the first he could find. "You'll slow me down."

Morigan scoffed.

Oenghus seized a better reason and bared his teeth when she turned to wait. "I need you to guard the— nymph from these bloody zealots. Make sure they don't leave without me."

"The nymph belongs to the Emperor," she reminded.

"We'll see about that," he growled.

"Are you planning on running off with her?"

"I didn't say that."

"But you thought it," she surmised. "*Think*, Oen, please. If you go home with a stolen nymph, the Blessed Order will follow. Despite our daughter's current disapproval of you, I doubt she'll turn on you outright, but as the Clans Head of Nuthaan, siding with you could be worse. The clans might not agree with her decision to support you. Either way, we'll have another war on our hands—be it an internal clans war or one with Kambe and the Blessed Order. Nuthaan will be defending three borders."

The kinsmen locked eyes. There were twelve years of recent war between them, of blood and slaughter and the screams of the dying. The paladins reached the Nuthaanians in the corridor, entering a tense silence.

"Think on that with the brain in your skull and not the one under your kilt," Morigan whispered, placing a hand on his arm. Oenghus nodded, squeezed her hand, and stepped away, turning to face the Inquisitor.

"What did the nymph say?"

"That I need to stop the taint," he told Ashe. Before she could question him further, he pushed his way through to the main hall, where the men were waiting. Ashe followed him out.

"You plan to go now?"

"Yes."

"With how many men?"

"Me," he grunted, planting himself in front of Gaborn. He held out a demanding hand, waiting for his war hammer and weapons.

"That's suicidal, Oenghus," Gaborn said.

"I'm a berserker," he rumbled.

"Do you know where the gorge is, or for that matter, where it all began?" Morigan's question gave him pause. He shifted, tugged his beard, and gestured in a northernly direction. Morigan sighed. There was years' worth of sighing in that sound.

The Inquisitor and Knight Captain conferred briefly. Ashe's eyes darted towards Oenghus, and when their heads came up, Keeling announced his plans to go.

"We'll take Farin as well—he knows where the tree is."

"Fine," Oenghus grumbled. "But I don't want to be caught out there at nightfall. Speed is our only chance."

Keeling nodded his agreement, and began shedding the heavier portions of his armor. He turned to his underling. "Fetch Sgt. Farin."

When the three were assembled and prepared, Morigan moved to Farin first, summoned the Lore and traced an intricate bind carefully over his boots. As the haggard scout shifted uncomfortably, she moved to the next man, repeating the process over Knight Captain Keeling. And finally, Oenghus.

After she tapped his boots, Morigan placed a bracing hand on the ground; weaving had sapped her strength. Oenghus helped her stand.

"Wait," she said. Before Oenghus could protest, she traced an armor weave and touched his throat. The familiar sensation of hardening skin spread over his body like a cloak. The healer swayed on her feet and coughed into her hand. There was blood on her palm.

"Damn you, woman," he growled.

"I'll be fine."

"Gaborn," Oenghus barked. The captain hopped to the healer's side.

"I'm not about to faint." Morigan waved Gaborn away, and looked at Oenghus. "Come back with blood on your shield, and if you don't, then piss in the ol'River for me. Enjoy yourself, Oen." She slapped his arse for good measure and he bared his teeth at the familiar send off. "I'll watch her," she reassured, turning towards the stairway, only steadying herself once on Gaborn's arm.

"Stubborn woman," he muttered at her retreating bun. Oenghus Saevaldr swallowed his concern for both women, shouldered his targe, touched his sacred flask, and strode out of the temple with a Knight captain and scout on his heels.

7

THE TAINT

OENGHUS SAEVALDR RAN over the dead ground, the hills and slopes and the cracks in the earth. He ran from another life. And he raced towards one. Heart pumping, blood rushing, muscles stretching. He moved with the speed of a stallion and the stamina of an Auroch—a god among men, racing the sun.

The Nuthaanian hopped onto a grouping of large boulders and surveyed the skeleton trees. White mountains surrounded the bleak valley and the wind whipped from their peaks, cooling his skin.

A long rent in the earth wound its way north, slicing through the valley floor like a crack of lightning. Nothing stirred in the desolation except the waxy ground, roiling and bulging as if a restless beast were on the verge of hatching. Oenghus did not like the image that thought conjured. Eventually, maggots morphed into flies; what would these larger ones turn into? He tugged on a braid, and glanced over his shoulder. Keeling and Farin were dim dots on the horizon.

Impatient, he traced the runes on his war hammer,

Gurthang, as he followed the gorge with his eyes. It reminded him of a Fjord—flush against a glacier's base, all tumbled and mixed with ice and earth from a recent landslide. Oenghus wondered what he would find in the bottom of the crevice.

Amid the forest of twisted deadwood, one lonely pine stood tall and white over the rest: the tree that Farin had pointed out from the ridge. Oenghus could wait—should wait—but he was restless. Irritated beyond words. The Sylph had asked the impossible of him and he needed to bash something before he exploded. The berserker was not known for his patience, nor for his ability to stand aside and wait for others.

With wild abandon, he jumped from the boulder and sprinted down the slope towards the tall pine, feeling a stir of rage, a blind focus, a bloody haze—the now and nothing beyond.

The gorge was a scar on the land, like all the scars across the realms that had swallowed countless lives during the Shattering. He skirted its edge, glancing into its depths. The sun was pale and angled, far too weak to illuminate the blackness at the bottom, but it did touch the sides, revealing a mottled patchwork of black earth and stone.

Oenghus slowed to a trot, eyeing the tree ahead. The ancient, and now dead, pine had held the essence of Life in its woody womb, and had birthed the Sylph into this realm—a different body, but the same spirit. The berserker shuddered at the thought of her vulnerability and of the danger to all that her presence brought. If something were to happen to her—not to the body, but to her spirit—the consequences would be far worse than the Shattering. Oenghus swallowed the fear, making it his own, and channeled it towards the pine.

The wood bulged and rippled as if it were alive. It would be ripe for the Void to feed on, even on a mere memory of the Sylph's presence.

Oenghus unhooked his hammer and began to chant with a voice that rumbled like thunder. The runes on his war hammer flared and he raised it with a shout, as he sped towards the base of the white pine. He swung. Electrifying power slammed into the wood with a crack that rebounded off the watching mountains.

The tree burst. And Oenghus raised his shield as the sky turned black, blotting out the sun. The Spawn burst into the open air—to the light of day—and were suspended in time for a heartbeat, until gravity caught them up, and sent the maggots hurling back towards earth. Thousands of wiggling carrion battered the Nuthaanian's shield. Those that did not shrivel from sunlight slithered beneath a waxy shell of death.

The berserker lowered his targe, shook off the remains with a jerk, and roared the Lore as he swung his hammer against the base of the tree, channeling the untamed weave through the rune-etched head. The ground shook, the deadfall groaned, and with a final surge of strength, Oenghus Saevaldr charged the tree, slamming his shoulder against its base. The blow tipped the ancient pine off its foundations. The ground gave up its roots and its crown toppled towards the gorge. Ripped from the earth, the pine plummeted into darkness and stopped with a deafening crash, its crown wedged against the opposite side of the chasm.

In one smooth sweep, Oenghus swung his targe over his back, reversed his hammer grip, and leapt into the pit. Air reached out to grab the giant, an unbearable foe that swirled around him like a mad dervish. His boots hit bark, knees buckled, and he slid. He twisted, driving the hammer's spike into the fallen tree. The spike shredded and slipped and then caught, jerking his shoulder, but his grip held fast.

Oenghus dangled over nothingness. The air was dark and cold, and if not for the sliver of sunlight high overhead, he would have thought himself blind. Gritting his teeth, he heaved, pulling his bulk towards the slanted tree. He reached up with his left, and searched. There, a knot. He hooked a finger into the hold and pulled himself up, scrambling onto the swaying trunk.

With a twist, he wrenched the spike from the bark and balanced on a precarious bridge, and, half slipping, half sliding, he made his way towards the opposite side of the chasm.

The top of the pine was wedged in a crevice. On this side of the divide, there were no maggots, no waxy earth—no sign of the taint. On the far side, however, the Spawn was drawn like moths to a flame, thirsting for the Goddess of All.

Oenghus hooked his hammer on his belt and gripped the rock wall with hands that had been hewn from granite. As long as there was a crevice, an edge, or even friction, his strength held. He climbed down, moving swiftly from one handhold to the next, until he came to a vertical crack in the cliff face. It was as good as a ladder to the Nuthaanian. He curled his fingers, making a fist, and wedged a hand into the crack. One fist after another, rapidly climbing down into nothingness until his boot touched a flat rock.

This far down, the temperature had plummeted with

the earth and the sun was as slender as a crescent moon above. Trickling water and the creaking of ice reached his ears. A frozen river.

Oenghus unslung his targe, slipped an arm through the straps and flexed, tucking his shield arm close to his body. As he let his eyes adjust to the dim light, he drew *Gurthang.* He had a hunter's sight that rarely failed him in the night. But even down here, in the depths of the earth with sunlight so distant, foliage grew. Darkwood glowed softly red in the gloom. Black leaves greedily soaked what little light bled through the crack above, and on this side of the river, the stunted trees thrived. The other side of the bank was lost to his sight.

Oenghus moved upriver, towards the mountains, and the recent avalanche. The sharp scent of decay crawled down his throat, sitting heavily in his stomach, tugging relentlessly at his innards. It was rot and death, and he followed the stench as he climbed over the rocky bank. The darkwood illuminated a curving shape, it looked like towering claws.

He stopped, studying the shape, trying to make sense of the shadows in the red glow. A slurping, sucking, hungry sound insinuated itself between the creak of ice.

All at once, his mind clicked, and he took a step back. The shapes were not claws, but ribs—a ribcage of monstrous proportions. And the Spawn was crawling over the half-buried carcass. Something seeped down the ribs like ooze and a shadow slowly took form—not the boulder he had thought it was at first, but a skull— the skull of a fiend. The source of the taint.

Oenghus held himself very still.

The bones moved, rock shifted, and a tremor roiled under the intruder's boots. Ever so slowly, Oenghus took a step back. And then another. An icy blue glow lit the crevice like a beacon as a single eye flared to life in the socket of a gruesome visage. The tainted sought life, but the Void consumed the spirit, and although ancient, Oenghus' spirit was strong and full of life. The Void sensed his presence.

The Spawn swarmed over the skull, slithering under the tattered remains of flesh, wrapping around bone like sinew. The massive jaws snapped shut. The sound filled his ears and stole his breath. The earth trembled as the skeletal fiend shifted and stirred, rising with a slow purposeful grate.

A towering, undead foe filled the crevice, shaking loose ice and rock. Oenghus did what any self-respecting berserker would do—he uncorked his flask and took a long, bold swig. Fire sped through his veins, searing his bones until the blood in his body threatened to burst from his pores. A roar ripped from his throat and the berserker slammed his hammer against shield, sparking lightning.

The Void-tainted fiend moved with a swarm of maggots, scraping the river of ice with its jagged bones. Oenghus charged the monstrosity. Lightning crackled in the gorge, blasting an appendage. Maggots flew into the air, but reformed as he reached the base, swinging his hammer at a leg. Calling it a leg was laughable. The spirit of the fiend did not care what shape it took or what bone it used—as long as it devoured.

Oenghus pounded his hammer into the monster, beating back blows and catching others on his targe. The realm narrowed until only a moment existed in the red haze of battle.

A strike blind-sided the berserker. He flew through

the air and hit stone. Instinct propelled him to the side, and he moved, throwing himself off an overhang as a massive hoof slammed into the rock. A sword sized talon came down, and he caught it on his shield. The screech of metal filled his ears, wood splintered, and the fiend drew back, ripping the shield from his arm.

Blood filled his senses. His forearm throbbed, and he let the pain feed his fury. Oenghus gripped *Gurthang* with both hands as an appendage whipped towards him. He cracked the head of the hammer into a crushing femur, batting it back. The bone shattered from the impact.

Again, Oenghus struck the fiend. The Swarm regrouped, reformed, and the fiend sprouted eight limbs that moved like tentacles. All of them struck at once, driving Oenghus back, step by precarious step, as he cleaved and hewed, straining to stay on his feet—until his back hit stone. Four bone tentacles stood poised, rattling like a snake, gathering strength for the final strike. With a rush of air, the fiend drove its limbs at the berserker.

Oenghus dove, felt the bite of razors and the pound of air. The chasm shook as the tentacles pierced the rocky wall. He threw his arms around the nearest limb, gripping the spiny vertebrae before it jerked upwards. When it did, he was yanked off his feet and *Gurthang* slipped from his bloody hands.

All was a blur, and all was pain as the tentacle sought to dislodge him, slamming him against the cliff. He held tight, ignoring the maggots swarming over his flesh, searching for a kink in his armor weave. As he rose ever higher, towards the fiendish skull, Oenghus roared the Lore and the Gift surged through his hands, sending a shockwave pulsing into the bones. The maggots withered and shrank back, abandoning the bones. The tentacle on which he clung collapsed.

Oenghus hit the frozen river with a crack. He surged to his feet, racing towards the fiend's legs and seized the closest, climbing up the thick bone with a surge of speed. Claws raked at the pest, tearing flesh, but Oenghus was lost in the haze of bloodlust, and every blow only fueled his rage. He reached the ribs and climbed inside the cage, slipping on carrion. A shriveled, decaying hide draped the remaining innards like a sagging tent. With a shout, Oenghus sent a bolt of lightning into the center of rot. It sizzled, the maggots recoiled, and, for a moment, a pale heart pulsed in his line of sight. Blackness oozed from the dead flesh.

Without weapon or shield, Oenghus was yet far from helpless. He gripped the end of a rib and heaved. It resisted. A slice of heat ripped down his back. The pain was enough. Muscles bulged, and with a roar, the rib snapped. He stumbled back, catching himself on a knob of bone. Oenghus hurled another bolt towards the heart of the fiend, lighting a tunnel with energy, opening a path through the tainted carrion. At the same instant, he drew back his arm, and brought it forward, hurling the sliver of bone.

The pointed rib fragment struck the heart, and Oenghus' world heaved as the fiend spasmed. The Swarm converged, seeking to protect what was most vulnerable—the source, the last remnant of the Void-tainted fiend.

As the monster thrashed, Oenghus leapt from the carcass, hit the ice, and slid. He scrambled and slipped as the bone fiend stabbed its pinchers in fury. In the darkness, amid the fading spark of its spirit still clinging to this realm, Oenghus' fingers closed around a familiar haft. Runes flared to life at his touch, and he stood, turning to face his towering foe. With a roar that shook the cliffs, he drove his hammer into the ice. A splinter turned into a crack, and then two, the ice fractured, cracks spreading like a spider's web from the focal point of power.

The frozen river gave way as the bone fiend clawed and thrashed for purchase, finding nothing to support its weight. It fell into the water. Oenghus ran, leaping from one island of ice to the next, striving to keep his balance. One slip, one misstep, and he would plunge into the deep Fjord with the fiend.

Icy water splashed on his leg, and the world fell from under his feet. He leapt, hit solid stone, and rolled. Without pause, he stood, turned to the cliffs and called to the mountain above—to the ancient stone. His booming voice stirred the earth like a quake. The rock recognized the life that had been hewn from its own by a crack of lightning, and responded. Boulders tumbled, and the great glaciers above shifted, thundering from the heights, falling into the chasm and slamming into the Void-fiend, driving it into the depths of the dark river.

When the roar had subsided, and its echo died, Oenghus Saevaldr stood in silence, gazing at the churning water. Summoning his strength, he raised his hands and brought them together with a booming clap. The sides of the chasm crumbled, filling the river, burying the Void-fiend beneath a mountain of earth.

8

BETRAYAL

A STREAK OF lightning reached out of the chasm towards the sky and a roar burst into the valley, shaking the ground beneath Farin Thatcher's feet. He scrambled away from the gorge, from the broken tree, and would have run all the way back to the castle, if it had not been for Knight Captain Keeling's hand clamping down on his shoulder.

"We're not going down there, are we?" Farin's voice was not as steady as he would have liked. Only a madman would venture into a Scar.

"Haven't you heard the saying, Sergeant?" Keeling asked. The Knight Captain's voice was as cool as iron. "Never follow a berserker. We have another mission."

"What might that be, sir?"

"The witch you found—she's enchanted the Nuthaanian. He is not right in his head."

Were berserkers ever right in the head? Farin kept his mouth shut. As if to emphasize this thought, the earth began to quake and a section of the chasm caved in by the mountain's base. The two men retreated, stumbling away from the edge. The earth did not relent. And thunder rumbled in their ears. It came from the pit, not the clear sky.

"But what about the taint?" Farin yelled over the rumbling.

"If the berserker stops it, then all the better."

"And if he doesn't?"

Keeling looked to Farin. "We have the other Wise One."

Farin looked away, towards the Scar. The Knight Captain was not suggesting that the kindly healer go down into the chasm—he was suggesting that they use her to leave the valley. As much as leaving appealed to Farin, he would not abandon his men.

"And what if he does?" he asked in a lull of shaking.

"We are to make sure that he does not return to the castle. Shoot on sight, Sergeant, and make good on your blunder. You should have never brought the witch into our midst."

Farin clenched his jaw, and nodded. And then they spoke no more, the earth roared, and both men were jarred from their feet. Farin fell onto the waxy earth and nearly lost his stomach as the Swarm responded to the touch of his unwarded skin. He scrambled upright as if he had been burnt, and staggered to a grouping of rocks that sat like an island in a sea of bleakness.

A slab cracked from the mountain and a great avalanche of ice and rock tumbled into the gorge. Farin could only watch, praying to the Guardians that the ground did not open up under his feet and swallow him whole. He feared the worst, as the surrounding earth ruptured like a bloated corpse, exposing the innards to daylight. Farin lost his stomach to the stench. But it did not last long: the Spawn shriveled and dried beneath the sun.

When silence had settled on the valley, Farin opened his eyes. He found himself clinging to a boulder like a cat on a log in the middle of a river. Ice and earth swirled in the air. He coughed, squinting through the hazy afternoon.

The ground was no longer writhing. It was still dead, but not like before. It looked more like dry earth in a water-starved land. Farin let out a slow, controlled breath, relieved that he was still able to breathe, but more so that they would not have to kill the Nuthaanian. Surely, the giant had been buried under the mountain?

Keeling and Farin waited nearly an hour for the ground to stop its restless shuddering. When it finally stilled for a good long while, Knight Captain Keeling stepped from the rocks and moved cautiously towards the Scar. Reluctantly, Farin followed, wondering if anyone had ever advised against following a Knight Captain of the Blessed Order.

The chasm was still black, but its shape had changed. Its edges were wider than before. As Keeling scanned its innards, Farin walked back to where this nightmare had begun—to the now toppled pine. Its roots had been ripped from the ground, and he could just make out the fallen tree's outline, wedged down in the gorge, spanning its width. It looked as though a giant had taken a bite out of the chasm's edge; only a sink hole remained where the majestic pine had once stood.

The earth was churned and the Spawn had already turned to ash beneath the sun. Color caught the sergeant's eye. A sliver of green in the center of the crater—a tiny bud of life amid the desolation. Farin's eyes widened. Another sprig emerged from the earth, and a third, uncurling, reaching towards the cold light. The buds unfolded and pale winter blossoms quivered with new life.

The sergeant gaped. But a distant grunt distracted him from wonder. The noise came from the gorge, between Keeling and himself. Farin notched an arrow, and peered cautiously into the blackness. A shadow moved. He could hear its labored breath, panting like a wounded bear. Small rocks were knocked loose and a muttered oath named the shadow. A moment later, the berserker climbed into the light, moving swiftly up the wall.

A bloodied hand slapped the top. With a growl, the berserker pulled himself over the edge, rolling onto solid ground. Oenghus lay on his back, panting. He was battered and broken and covered in ichor. Dazed and utterly unaware, the giant's chest heaved, he groaned, and rolled onto all fours hacking up blood.

Farin drew back his string at the same moment that the Knight Captain moved forward with drawn sword. In one practiced motion, Keeling brought his sword up like an executioner's axe.

Time is a strange thing. For Farin Thatcher—time slowed. He was aware of every breath, every flurry dancing with a smote of ash; he heard the shift of armor and the slice of air. The soldier could see the Nuthaanian reacting with what seemed like glacier speed. But most of all, Farin saw the trio of blossoms that had unfurled their white petals like sails after a storm. Without thought, Farin loosed his arrow.

Time surged. The arrow zipped, and the blade came down. Thatcher's arrow pierced Keeling through the eye and ended in his brain. The force of the shot knocked Keeling off-kilter, his blade went wide, slicing a trail down the barbarian's prone back instead of through his neck.

The Knight Captain fell down dead. And Farin Thatcher froze, shocked at his own split-second choice. The kilted berserker turned his head and looked at Farin with an eye that chilled his blood. Oenghus grabbed the paladin's sword and staggered to his feet. He let the tip of the sword rest on the earth where he stood swaying and panting, gathering his strength.

Berserkers were notorious for cutting down friend and foe alike. But Farin was no longer frightened, he was petrified as realization slammed fully into his muddled mind—he had disobeyed orders, and murdered a Knight Captain of the Blessed Order. By the gods, he'd be better off throwing himself over the edge and have a quick clean death. Let the gorge take him. The Blessed Order was notorious for its drawn-out executions.

Farin did not know what to do. He wanted to run, but feared the berserker would charge if he moved. Blazing, sapphire eyes held Farin rooted in place, and the giant raised his sword, looking like a fiendish guardian standing at the Gates of the Nine Halls.

"Keeling said you were bewitched," Farin said, dropping his bow and raising his hands.

"What do you think?" the berserker rasped like Death herself.

"The flowers," he blurted unintelligibly. He turned and pointed at the dainty, impossible trio that had now blossomed into a dozen. Nothing evil would give birth to life.

The berserker bared his teeth, stark white against

the black of his beard. "So there are, lad, so there are." He tossed the sword away from him as if it were Blighted, giving it to the chasm. Oenghus nudged the Knight Captain with his boot. "Did this bastard have orders?"

Farin nodded.

"Thought so," he grunted, and gave the corpse a good kick, sending it sprawling into the gorge. The paladin disappeared. "Too bad you didn't get those orders before the honorable Knight Captain's unfortunate accident, aye?"

The visions of torture faded away. The soldier nodded, and he finally remembered to breathe.

9

REUNION

"WHERE IS MY Knight Captain?" the Inquisitor asked at the gates without preamble. For the first time in weeks, the castle's survivors stood on the walls savoring the moonlight. Their torches burned brightly in the night, illuminating the towering, blood-covered Nuthaanian and his makeshift bandages.

"He fell," Oenghus grunted, and leaned in close. "Here is a thought, Inquisitor: who else are you going to trust to get the nymph safely to Whitemount? Are you and your twitchy acolyte and mindless blade going to escort her alone, or worse, surrounded by an army of battle-weary Kamberian men?"

He waited.

"You gave your word," she said at length.

"I did. And a Nuthaanian never has to give his word twice. I'm your best chance of getting the finder's reward for the nymph. Are we clear?"

The Inquisitor inclined her head.

"You're welcome," he growled. Without another word, he brushed by Ashe, spitting on the ground to rid himself of her presence. As the Nuthaanian strode through the courtyard, the occupants who were burying the bones paused to cheer the hero.

Gaborn Oakstone smiled at Oenghus and clapped him on the shoulder. "You look like a dead man walking."

"Don't I always?" he grunted.

"What happened?" the captain asked.

"Nasty, is what. Watch my back, Gaborn. The bloody Knight Captain tried to separate my head from its neck. I like it where it is."

Gaborn's eyes slid towards the frowning Inquisitor. "Orders?"

Oenghus nodded, and Gaborn muttered something rude under his breath. After twelve years of fighting, there was little love between the Blessed Order and the soldiers of Kambe. Their Knight Captains had no qualms about sending men to their deaths for an inch of ground gained.

"But why would she want you dead?"

"Fear," Oenghus rumbled. "She's worried I'll take the nymph."

Gaborn's eyes widened. "The witch is a nymph?"

"Aye, keep it under your helm, understand?"

"I'll have to inform the Field Marshal when the army arrives."

"As long as he is prepared to organize all the women soldiers… quiet-like. We have a long march back to Whitemount."

"Are you planning on coming with us?"

Oenghus did not answer, instead he sighed, "Where's Morigan?"

"In the garden with the—nymph."

A GUARD STOOD in front of the archway that led into a walled garden, the same helmeted paladin who had guarded the temple. The woman was tall and she blocked the pathway with her bulk. Oenghus stopped in front of the paladin, turned back to the Inquisitor and jerked his head. At the Inquisitor's gesture the guard stepped aside.

The walled garden was already overgrown. Yasine's mere presence had renewed life. But before he could find the Sylph, Morigan found him.

"By the gods—" she caught herself, steadied her voice, and said, instead, "You're a mess, Oen."

"I'm fine, Mori."

"Well, you're walking, aren't you?" she sighed, eyeing his wounds. "You do like to make me work, don't you?"

He bared his teeth—the only clean bit on him.

"Thank you," a voice said from the shadows. Oenghus was not surprised. Even before she spoke, he could sense Yasine, knew she was content and pleased with his deed. A moment later, the Sylph emerged from darkness into moonlight, and for a heartbeat, bathed in the silver light of her own moon, she appeared in her true silver-eyed form. Morigan's breath caught. But the vision was fleeting—easily dismissed as a trick of the eye.

Yasine glided closer.

"Step away from him," Ashe snapped as she marched into the garden. "Bring the nymph inside the temple," she ordered the large paladin at her side.

A low growl rumbled from Oenghus' throat, but a flash of green eyes stilled his intent. Yasine looked meekly at the earth and followed the Inquisitor willingly. When they were alone, Morigan gripped his arm. He winced, and she loosened her hand, glaring at the offending wound.

"You can tell me what the Void is going on while I put you back together."

Oenghus grunted, and gave himself over to Morigan's will, feeling like a helpless coward. The Sylph's plea rang in his ears: *stand still and do not react.*

With efficiency, Morigan commandeered a private room, ordered fresh linens, hot water, and handed off his kilt to be laundered and mended—as if the castle had nothing better to do. But in one day, Morigan had restored the chain of command, and brought order to the survivors. There was no disheartened, disordered, leaderless army that stood a chance against the healer's calming presence.

Oenghus, like so many others, surrendered to her competent hands. This worried Morigan to no end. She stood by the bed, frowning at the blood soaked bandages on his back and shield arm and the cuts that were not bandaged. He shifted on his stomach to eye her. The lines of exhaustion had not left.

"Just get the back and arm. The rest will heal with your salve." It was a testament to her state that she did not argue. But Morigan did not immediately set to work, she planted her backside on the bed.

"Before I start—what's going on? Rotting Void fiends don't turn up every day." And while they waited for water and linens, Oenghus sketched over the details of the battle and the subsequent betrayal of the Knight Captain.

"I figure the carcass was probably frozen in the mountains, likely slain during the Era of Blight and left to rot," he murmured. "I think the earthquakes must have knocked it loose and the air warmed enough to thaw it out in the chasm."

"I'm not an idiot," she interrupted, firmly. "You know what I'm getting at. The *nymph*, Oen. Who is she to you?"

"I've said all I can, Mori." There was a plea in his voice that alarmed her, but long-time companions that they were, she pressed the issue as she usually did.

"I've healed two nymphs, and I've never seen one make trees grow like she did in that garden, and those eyes of hers, in the moonlight—"

"There's always a first time," he pointed out.

Morigan snorted. "And I've been with, on, and under you enough to know more than I should about you."

He chuckled at her words.

"Is she who I think she is?"

"I've never been able to change your bull-headed mind once you get an idea settled in there."

"At least you've learned one thing in all these years," she retorted. When Oenghus did not rise to the bait of an argument, Morigan placed a comforting hand on his muscled shoulder. It gave him the strength to make a choice.

"I won't be going home, Mori. I'll travel on to Whitemount."

To his surprise, she nodded as if she'd suspected it already. "Then I'll be going, too."

Oenghus turned slightly. Dark, familiar eyes stared down at him with more love than he deserved. "Why?" he asked.

"In all these years—through our three Oaths," she whispered. "I've never seen you look so trapped, Oen."

"You should also know by now not to worry about my hairy hide."

"Someone has to, you big oaf," she smiled, and bent forward to place a kiss on his temple.

"What would I do without you, Mori?" he murmured.

"Probably bleed to death."

A SOLID WALL of snow blocked his path. Oenghus was trapped. Howling filled his ears, making his prison unbearable. The screams were feral and pleading and all consuming. It came from his Oathbound, his very first. She was ripe with child—their child who could not find its way out. She was dying, and with snow all around there was nothing he could do. Her cries pushed at the walls of their cabin and beat at his ears. There was no help, nowhere to go. He was as trapped and helpless as she; alone, he sat watching his Oathbound and child die.

Consciousness saved him this time. Oenghus Saevaldr sat bolt upright in the night. He threw off the covers and leapt to his feet, ready to fight. There he stood, panting like a caged lion. However, he was alone.

A warm hearth mingled with the moonlight, a silver stream that slipped through the narrow window. There was no danger, no other one there, save the howling of a dream and the memory of a helpless twenty-year-old fool who had never done anything useful but bash heads. And now, over nine hundred years later, he still felt like that fool—trapped and helpless, unable to aid those he loved.

That did not set well with Oenghus. He snatched his belt from a pile of belongings and uncorked his grog, taking a long swig. The Brimgrog burned away his memories, centered him in the now, and filled his veins with fire. A growl rumbled from deep inside his chest and he drove his fist into the mantel, cracking the stone.

His hand hurt, but he welcomed the simplicity of pain. The heart was never so straightforward.

"I didn't gift you with a bottomless supply of Brimgrog so you could guzzle it like a drunkard."

Oenghus spun, muscles tensing for battle a moment before his mind recognized the voice. The Sylph—Yasine as he alone called her—stood in the center of moonlight. Green eyes roved appreciatively over his body; muscle and power draped in firelight and shadow. He could feel her need, her desire, amplified by his own.

Yasine moved like water, flowing across the floor to stand within reach. "Swear to me," she said.

Her voice made him hard, her presence filled him, and he seized her. The Sylph went willingly. She wrapped her arms around his neck and her lips met his with equal hunger. It had been so long. The lovers trembled, aching, fumbling in their desperation. Coarse, strong hands tugged her robe free, and flung it to the far side of the room. He slid his hands down her back, relishing her curves, her warmth, and the press of her body against his. He gripped her backside and lifted. Strong thighs wrapped around his waist.

Frantic moments passed as Oenghus sought the bed. The realm tilted. And the Sylph spread her thighs, welcoming what she could not control—the only man she had ever loved. He was everything opposite; hard and coarse and impatient.

Oenghus gripped her flank and filled her with unyielding power. His growl mingled with her gasp, and she nipped his ear with her teeth. She was all softness and heat and he sank into her with a shuddering sigh, and for a moment, they simply lay intertwined. Oenghus raised himself on his elbows, sparing her his weight, pulling back to meet her eyes. She smiled, relishing the heat of him, the thickness pulsing inside until she could stand it no longer.

"Swear to me," she breathed, clenching her muscles around his shaft. Oenghus grunted, and thrust, rendering her speechless. He tasted her neck and she arched her back. When his lips locked over a hard nipple, she gasped, and pushed, rolling him to the side so she came out on top. Precisely where she liked to be. A primal chorus of moans entered the room as the united lovers reacquainted themselves, until they moved as one, in a timeless rhythm.

It did not last long.

He could feel her muscles tensing, the slight trembling that turned into a quaking, until her body stiffened and her lips parted with a cry. He grabbed her neck, and brought her lips to his, silencing her ecstasy. She moaned into his mouth. She was utter bliss and happiness and the violence of her release drove him over the precipice. His shaft throbbed and he groaned as she met his hips with her own.

Through the hazy aftermath, he watched her shapely, swaying form, riding him until she had had her fill twice over. With her desire stilled, she slipped off and slid to the side, as limp and satiated as her lover.

They lay for a long time, half-intertwined, her head over his heart, her fingers idly drifting through the hair on his chest as she traced the muscles of his body, learning his lines anew.

Oenghus ran one hand over the thigh draped across his own, and with the other, brushed Yasine's back, letting his touch drift downwards to rest on her backside.

"I thought you couldn't use your power?" he murmured in the quiet. His breath stirred her hair and he inhaled her scent, the calm after the storm.

"I see your mind is working again." He felt her lips curve.

"Not for very long." To emphasize his words, he gripped a handful of sumptuous flesh and rolled onto his side, taking her with him. Her head dropped to his bicep and she stared into his eyes. Green met blue; like the sea and the land watching each other, breathing the same air.

"Moonlight," she said softly, brushing the unruly hair from his eyes. "There is always power in the moon's light. I can step from one pool to the next."

"Like a teleportation rune," he surmised.

"Something like that, yes." There was a knowing glint in her eyes. "Trees, too."

"I've seen the Scarecrow do that."

"Once upon a time, in another age, you could do the same with stone."

A flash of pain stabbed his temple, and he winced.

"I'm sorry, my love," she soothed, brushing the spot as if the pain were her own, which it was—what one felt, the other sensed. "I won't mention such things."

"I'll not be coddled," he growled.

"You let Morigan tend to you," she retorted.

"She healed me." He narrowed his eyes. "Are you jealous? She and I haven't been Oathbound for near a century."

"Yet her bed is not unfamiliar to you." Yasine toyed with one of the braids in his beard. He opened his mouth, but fell silent at a twinkle in her eye "Why would I be jealous of a woman who has taken three Oaths with you? A woman who has born your children? How can I feel anything but gratitude towards Morigan, who loves and cares for you when I cannot?"

For Oenghus, who had spent the majority of this life in ignorance, the long separation was not as keen, but he could feel the ache in the Sylph's heart.

"I like Morigan," she smiled. "I always have. She is one of my favored in this realm and one of the few who has put up with you. Not an easy feat."

"It's my cock."

She laughed, a musical, wonderful sound that bridged the years. Oenghus let himself remember the last time he had heard her laugh, and his heart ached. As he had that day, in another Age, of another name, he never wanted to let her go—never wanted to leave their bed. With mist in his eyes, he cupped her face, tracing the curve of her ears, as she nuzzled her forehead against his beard. His chest shuddered with control.

"You know I can't stay in this realm long," she breathed, lips brushing his skin, her tears mingling with his. "As you said, every day is a risk."

"Then why risk yourself at all?"

"I've told you."

"A child, yes—and nothing else."

"Do you remember the first time you spoke to me?"

For her, he spoke the words of another: the dead god whose spirit resided in his flesh. "*I am the lightning, I am the crag and the rocks and the raging storms. I am the sea and its roar.*"

When his voice grew gruff with pain, she finished for him, "*I am passion and fire, and everything you cannot control.*" Her fingers brushed through his hair, soothing the pain in his heart. "Your spirit is worn, my love. Although formidable, you are but a shadow of what you once were. And yet, still, after all these Ages, from one life to the next, I cannot tame you."

Oenghus untangled himself from her embrace, and sat up. "But you come and you tell me not to act—to stand aside. You ask the impossible," he snarled.

He felt her rise. A gentle hand touched his back, as light as a feather's brush on his recent injuries. "I do not ask it for myself, Oenghus. I ask it for our child. I have made many mistakes. The more I try to interfere, the more I fight the Void, the worse it becomes. You were not here for the Shattering—for our daughter's death." He cocked his head, as if the tilt would dislodge a memory. But the veil remained. "Your spirit was greatly damaged after your fight with Karbonek. I feared you would not return, and you did not, for many, *many* long years." Though he did not turn, he could hear the tears in her eyes, feel them falling down her cheeks as if they were his own.

"Karbonek," he tasted the name, but no memory came. It was frustrating.

"Yes," she whispered. "The Void is powerful, it devours all Life. But Life cannot fight what consumes— so I must trust to what I cannot control. I must stand back and hope."

He looked at her then, where she sat cross-legged on their bed—exposed, vulnerable, and full of fear.

"Does the Scarecrow have anything to do with this?"

"By the Light—no," she breathed, closing her eyes. "Even if he were whole, I am sure he would disapprove and attempt to stop me. You must not tell him the child is mine."

Oenghus tugged on a braid. That, at least, gave him satisfaction. Currently he had a bone to pick with the ol' bastard. "So this isn't some bloody prophecy?"

"It is a thought—a last desperate hope."

"So you can't control me?" he growled, and moved towards her on all fours. Yasine fell back, settling herself on the mattress between his arms and legs. "What is stopping me from knocking you over the head and carrying you away as I once did?"

She sighed. "To where? Nuthaan? And spend my pregnancy in a freezing cabin—hunted by the Blessed Order and Void, living in fear that our daughter might fall into Wedamen hands? Absolutely not, Oenghus," she said firmly with a shake of her head. "If I'm going to carry your child, then let me do it in warm luxury."

"What of the Emperor?"

"Many children are born prematurely," she lifted a shoulder.

"You'll be his—as a nymph."

"You are not the only man I have shared my bed with," she reminded. "If the Emperor thinks she is his child, then she will be protected. Aside from Iilenshar, Kiln and Kambe are the most powerful kingdoms in this realm. Kiln will crush her, and I'll not have a child of mine fall into the Guardians' hands again. That leaves Kambe."

"I don't like it."

"I don't either, but I had hoped you would enjoy keeping me company for nine months."

His eyes flickered to her stomach, all softness and curves, not the slim figure of a slip of a girl, but that of a woman—ripe and sumptuous. His body hardened, striving to reach her. "Do you have what you need already?"

Yasine stroked his shaft, fingers curling around its girth, gently tugging him to her. "I don't know. Everything from here on out is chance. You don't have to, my love," she purred. "I won't force myself on you."

Oenghus snorted, and lay to the side, cupping her breast, teasing her nipple to life as he kissed the curve of her neck. Her legs parted and his fingers touched the moist triangle of fine hair, moving towards heat.

"Swear to me," she gasped.

"Never," he growled in her ear.

WHITEMOUNT

IN THE DAYS that followed, a flurry of messengers and Whispers came and went. Kambe's army marched from the pass into the valley that was no longer dead, and made camp at the foot of the castle. Horses were brought, a female guard was organized, and with the usual efficiency of Kambe, the long line of war-weary solders marched home.

Yasine did not visit him again. She was guarded day and night, kept hidden beneath a veil, and placed in the midst of her honor guard. Much to his relief, Morigan stayed at her side. Inquisitor Ashe could not find any reason to dismiss the kindly healer who calmed the nymph. If not for Morigan's vigilance, Oenghus thought he would have gone mad.

Days became weeks, and their journey quickened when mountain passes gave way to the spacious stone roads of Kambe. A carriage was provided for Yasine, and fresh horses for her guard. Oenghus rode alongside as their company met with new soldiers from the Emperor's elite. The escort broke off from the main force and rode towards Whitemount. Emperor Soataen Jaal III eagerly awaited his nymph.

Whitemount crowned a hill, above the sea and fog, overlooking its domain from white walls and rising towers. Through the ages, many would-be conquerors had been deceived by its elegance, mistaking beauty for weakness. But Kambe's strength lay in its order and discipline, and save for the Shattering, its walls had never been breached.

As the escort climbed the winding road, the silver, blue, and white flags of Kambe swelled like sails. The fog parted, and a clear, sweeping view of the harbor lay at Oenghus' feet. But he only offered it a brief glance; his eyes were on the carriage that rolled steadily towards the palace. He could feel Yasine through their bond. She was serene and slightly irritated with him—for he was far from calm.

In all his long years, Oenghus had avoided setting foot in the Kambe palace, and he wasn't keen on doing so now. Royalty annoyed him at the best of times, and this occasion was far from joyous—he was about to place the woman he loved in another man's hands.

With a surge of anger, Yasine dropped a veil between their spirits, shoving him and his foul mood far away from her. Oenghus glared at the carriage as they rode through the gates. Going along with her scheme was one thing; being happy about it was quite another.

The palace courtyard gleamed with guards in all their finery. The regiment snapped to attention with a clap of steel as standards waved over a bailey of polished heads. As the carriage entered, the line of soldiers stepped neatly to the side, pressing fist to heart in salute: a king's welcome—or in this case, a queen.

The carriage settled in front of a waterfall of white steps. Grooms stepped forward, taking control of the horses, and Oenghus dismounted, flashing half the courtyard as he stepped down to the cobblestones. Kilts were not made for modesty.

Whitemount's towers did not match the Spine in height, but the arches and delicate lattice-work put the Wise Ones' tower to shame. Tearing his gaze from the curving beauty, he handed his reins to a groom, and patted his gelding in gratitude.

A dapper Chamberlain bowed to the Inquisitor, and Oenghus turned towards the soldiers, sizing them up. He ignored the useless court pleasantries and introductions—until he heard his name.

"What?" he demanded of the pointy-eared dandy.

"Lord Saevaldr, His Imperial Majesty, requests your presence, along with Lady Freyr."

"Aye, fine." Oenghus frowned, recounting all the generals, captains, and officials he had yelled at over the past twelve years. Morigan, however, was the one who had bullied the Field Marshal.

Ashe kept her face blank, but her eyes smoldered as she stepped towards the carriage, opening the door. Yasine stepped lightly down. The 'nymph' was unveiled, her auburn hair fell in waves over her shoulders and the silk robe of white she wore did little to conceal her lush outline. The air thickened and the hush could be heard. All eyes followed the ethereal creature as she glided up the steps in the company of her honor guard.

Oenghus offered his hand to Morigan and she accepted, climbing out of the carriage with little grace.

"You're a lady," he murmured.

She snorted.

"His Majesty wants to see us."

"Oh, Void." She nearly spat, but caught herself. Together, they walked up the stairs, following in Yasine's wake. "By the gods, try to behave yourself, and don't get me executed."

He bent down, so he could whisper loudly in her ear. "You're the one that gave the Marshal what-for."

"And I'd do it again."

He bared his teeth. "Always after my heart, aren't you?"

Morigan glanced sideways at him. "Your heart is otherwise occupied at the moment. Are you going to be all right?"

"Why would you ask that?"

"You have that certain look about you," she whispered. "Of a berserker about to rip someone's head off."

He grunted.

They stepped through the gates, into a resplendent great hall of white marble. Six Guardian statues flanked the entrance hall like pillars. Zahra, the Radiant, shining in golden armor; Chaim, the River God, draped in his white robes; Zemoch, the Stalwart, holding his double-headed flail; Asmara, the Everchild, who had not aged a day since the Shattering; Oshimi, the Serene, sitting cross-legged with his fingers joined; and finally, Yvesa, the Peaceful, a winged sprite. Beyond, through an impossible archway, the throne room and its multitudes were gathered.

"Remember, Oen, in Kambe, we are not only Wise Ones, but as the parents of the Clans Head, we represent Nuthaan, too. Whatever you do will reflect upon our daughter's honor, which has already been jeopardized once, thanks to you."

Of all the voices that could reason with the berserker, Morigan's got through the most. He tugged on his beard, trying not to think of their daughter who was rightly angry with him; instead, he nodded, and focused on Yasine. He could feel her again, and he soaked in her serene presence. Her spirit wrapped around his own like a caress, soothing and untroubled as a mountain lake.

It calmed his mind.

Like the great hall, the throne room shone white. The marble was polished to a reflective sheen, and the high windows bathed the sunburst throne at the end of the room in warm light. It was difficult to look at, nearly blinding.

Silk and lace and perfume assaulted Oenghus as the party walked through the sea of courtiers towards the throne. The colors of the Great Houses hung from the high ceiling like the great sails of a Mearcentian trade ship. Oenghus was unimpressed; his practical nature wondered how many people had wasted their lives embroidering the useless fabric so some lazy lord could get his twig up.

The Chamberlain's group stopped at the foot of the first dais. The Emperor's bodyguards, known as the Hounds, flanked the stairs. They stepped aside and Yasine was escorted up to the first dais by a woman in ceremonial armor.

Perched on his sunburst throne, Emperor Soataen Jaal III looked down from the second tier, studying his nymph to be. His hair was as golden as his throne and the diadem atop his head. With pointed ears and a noble bearing, he looked every bit a Kamberian. It was rumored that Lindale blood ran strong in his family's line. Oenghus had never put much stock in the rumors, but looking at the ruler now, in the flesh, he could not deny the stories. Soataen was tall and chiseled, with high cheekbones and striking blue eyes.

Oenghus might have placed him as a dandy lord, but there was intelligence in those eyes, and Soataen had a reputation as a just and fair ruler. His people loved him.

Currently, those eyes were locked upon Yasine—*his gift*. And then he stood, and all heads bowed, save the nymph's and the Nuthaanians'. Soataen stepped from his throne, joining Yasine on her dais. A murmur of anger rippled through the crowd. Oenghus figured it was his and Morigan's erect spines. But Nuthaanians bowed to no man or god, and the last ruler who had forced a Nuthaanian to do so had found a horde of berserkers on his doorstep.

"All may rise," the emperor's voice carried to the farthest reaches of the chamber. Backs straightened, and the audience's anger was soon forgotten as they watched their beloved emperor take the nymph's hand and bow over it with a brush of lips. Anger turned to surprise.

"Welcome to my palace, m'lady. My house is yours." His voice was strong, but kind. And in a lower voice, Oenghus heard the emperor inquire after her name. Yasine did not reply.

Soataen looked to the Inquisitor, still standing on the floor beside Oenghus. "Does she have a name?"

"I do not know, your majesty. The nymph has only spoken to the Nuthaanians."

A sharp eyebrow shot upwards. Soataen looked at the pair and Oenghus spoke up before the emperor could ask, breaking yet another rule. "She needs trees, a garden, lots of earth to roam." His voice rumbled like thunder in the hall, and the Hounds tensed at his breach of protocol.

Soataen raised a hand, silencing the murmur. His gaze returned to Yasine. "You shall have everything you desire. Please, go with my chancellor, she will see to all your needs."

Yasine inclined her head. The woman in ceremonial armor stepped forward, along with two female Hounds. They escorted the nymph through an archway off the second dais. A sea of heads turned, following her departure, including Soataen's.

When the nymph disappeared, the audience seemed to shake itself out of a dream. The emperor turned his attention to Inquisitor Ashe. He did not invite her onto his dais, nor did he return to his throne, but remained standing on the first tier.

"I received numerous reports on the taint in Northolt. It is well that such evil is vanquished. I mourn the lives lost. You have my gratitude, for preserving the life of the nymph when others wished her harm, Inquisitor Ashe."

"I thank you, your majesty. I upheld the Law of my sacred Order, nothing more."

"Indeed," he said. "And the Law rewards those who uphold it. Chamberlain Emerich will see to your reward."

Oenghus cleared his throat, loudly. And the Hounds twitched with threat. The emperor looked at him again. "Yes, Lord Saevaldr?"

The title grated on his ears, but he ignored it for now. "I think the Law states that the finder's fee for a nymph goes to the person who first found her—doesn't it, Inquisitor?"

Ashe frowned severely, but nodded.

"Well, I'd just like to point out that Sergeant Farin found her, didn't he?"

"Is this true?" the emperor asked.

"He did," the Inquisitor confirmed, "and brought her to the keep. He thought her a witch."

The emperor looked to his chamberlain. "See that the reward is split. That is all, Inquisitor Ashe."

The Inquisitor bowed low and stepped back, but not before she shot Oenghus a seething glare. His finger twitched, and he fought down the urge to offer the Inquisitor a pointed gesture.

The emperor motioned to his chamberlain, and the prim man looked to the Nuthaanians. "You may ascend the first dais."

Another murmur traveled through the audience as Morigan and Oenghus stepped up, the latter towering over the emperor.

"I welcome our allies of the north. Your deeds in the Wedamen war have reached my ears countless times. Lady Morigan Freyr, mother of the Clans Head of Nuthaan, you honor Kambe with your presence." He offered his shield arm, as was customary to all women in Nuthaan. Morigan gripped his forearm heartily.

"May Death find you with enemies at your feet, your majesty." And then, to show her appreciation for his knowledge of their customs, she curtsied to show her consideration of theirs.

"If I had ten generals with your mettle, Lady Freyr, I'd never have to make another ruling as long as I lived,"

Soataen smiled. And Oenghus felt a twinge of grudging respect for the emperor.

Morigan blushed. "I just help out where I see a need." She was so flustered that she forgot to add his title. In all their time together, Oenghus had rarely seen her blush.

To Oenghus, Soataen offered his sword arm, and the berserker gripped his forearm with an iron hand. "I know your name Oenghus Saevaldr," the emperor said.

"And I know yours Soataen Jaal," he returned.

The emperor's grip held no weakness. "Kambe owes you much for ridding the north of that vileness. To say nothing of your deeds during the war. My Field Marshal spoke highly of you. Grimstorm has become legend in my lands."

"Your soldiers fought hard," he said with honesty. "The honor goes to those who stood, and those who fell."

Silence blanketed the court. Many had died in the Wedamen war—many innocents. "Indeed," the emperor said at length. "But I wish to honor you both still, with title and land, and to you Oenghus Saevaldr, I offer a place in my court as Champion of Kambe."

Oenghus tugged on his beard. "That's generous, your majesty." He already had land, and he wanted to go back home to his own hearth. But Oenghus didn't voice his desire. "I've been fighting for twelve years straight—I'm tired of fighting." Morigan nearly choked; instead she coughed over his ridiculous claim. "I'm a Wise One, too, and first and foremost, a healer. If you have need of me as Wise One or healer, then I would be honored to serve."

Another ripple of whispers brushed his back.

"As Wise One you will stay, then," the emperor intoned. They clasped forearms, and Oenghus nodded, backing off the dais. "Lady Freyr, I am told that the nymph takes comfort in your presence. Would you honor us with yours until she is settled?"

"I'd be happy to, your majesty. As long as there's an infirmary that can use an extra pair of hands."

Matters settled, the emperor nodded to his chamberlain, and exited, walking through the archway. The moment he disappeared, along with his guards, the audience erupted with chatter. As an attendant stepped forward to escort the Nuthaanians to their rooms, Oenghus bumped shoulders with Ashe. "Go collect your bloody reward," he growled.

If he never saw another soldier of the Blessed Order as long as he lived, he would die a happy man.

OENGHUS PACED IN THE MOONLIGHT, back and forth across his balcony. It overlooked Wyrim's Fist, the great harbor of Kambe, and the sea beyond. As breathtaking as the view was, he longed for the snow covered crags of his homeland—an ache that was nearly as acute as his longing for Yasine.

A week had passed since their arrival. The days had been filled with banquets, feasting, a week-long celebration for the victorious soldiers. For the sake of Yasine, and in hopes of catching a glimpse of her, Oenghus had endured the court idiots, their flowery speech, and their prim little pointed ears; however, in the end, she had not attended a single banquet with the emperor. And while he was glad Soataen was not parading her around like a prize horse, he was also worried. Was she being kept in the palace under lock and key? A cage might be gilded, but it was still a cage.

If not for their bond, Oenghus would have stormed the emperor's private wing. He could, at least, sense Yasine's moods, and knew that she was content and safe.

Sensing his distress, Morigan reported daily, assuring Oenghus that Yasine was fine—that she had an entire wing of rooms, and that a walled garden was being extended so she might come and go as she pleased. So why hadn't Yasine come to him?

One moment, Oenghus was alone, and the next he was not. The Sylph stepped out of a pool of moonlight, and crossed her arms gracefully beneath her breasts. "Stop fretting. It's tiresome."

Oenghus did not hesitate; he swept Yasine off her feet and carried her to his bed. In the firelight, he made love to her, slow and purposeful, savoring every curve. When the lovers were spent, they lay intertwined in a tangle of bedding.

The flicker of flame caressed her naked flesh, playing with shadows beneath his eyes. Yasine idly combed his hair with her fingers, brushing the nape of his neck, and tracing the lines of powerful shoulders.

"My attendants have been overly attentive," she explained. "They didn't like me venturing into the garden at night. I had to convince them that I was safe and wanted to be alone—not an easy thing to do when one doesn't speak."

"And the emperor?"

"He comes daily, along with his children at times," she answered. "We eat in the garden and walk. Soataen talks while I tend to the trees and flowers. It is not an unpleasant way to spend my afternoons."

"It's dangerous playing the innocent."

"I am supposed to be a nymph," she raised a shoulder. "What other role would you have me play?"

"You are helpless as you are."

"Shall I tell the emperor that I'm the Sylph in disguise?"

"I didn't say that," Oenghus grumbled.

"Do not think that I am blind to how my nymphs are treated in this realm," she sighed. "Unfortunately, my power is diminished here, and in other realms. Still, I do what I can, but more often than not, I can only watch the abuses heaped upon them from my grove." Sadness filled her eyes, and her hand dropped to his beard, where she curled one braid around her finger. "Sometimes there is truth in legend, you know. And other times—most times—truth is sorely twisted. A nymph does not make men mad, Oenghus. Nymphs uncover what is already there. Man or god, an individual's true nature is revealed."

"Is that why you gave nymphs as gifts to the gods?"

Yasine's eyes grew distant, looking back over the Ages with sadness. "I've learned much about my *allies*."

He grunted.

Green eyes sharpened. "You think me cruel?"

"Cunning. Necessary perhaps, but not so fortunate for your army of unknowing spies."

"Nymphs live in the moment, Oenghus," she explained. "Give them a chocolate, or show them a butterfly, and all is forgotten. But…" she frowned in thought, "…even my nymphs changed during the Shattering."

"Didn't everything?"

"Not you." Yasine pressed her cheek against his, savoring the feel of his beard on her silken flesh. He kissed her throat, tasting the shiver that skipped down her spine. "Eventually, I will have to go to Soataen."

The kiss turned sour on his lips. Oenghus was Nuthaanian—women chose who and when and with as many men as they pleased. But there was no joy in Yasine's words. She was not eager to share the emperor's bed. It turned his stomach.

Sensing his unease, she tried to conceal her own. "Soataen is hardly repulsive. He is confident, possessed of an acrobat's body and grace—smooth and muscled— and clean shaven. I'll wager there isn't a hair on his chest." Yasine ran her fingers through the thick black hair that covered his own. "His hands are fine, not coarse as a rock. I shall enjoy him—he's everything opposite of you."

"You like every inch of me," he growled, pulling her on top.

"All nine," she quipped.

He bared his teeth, and she slid down his body, appreciating every inch until he forgot about the future, her words and his worry, and even his name.

THE LESSON

Thawing, 1993 A.S.

EMERALD HILLS ROLLED like waves to the sea. A strong breeze cooled the sun as a group of riders meandered over a crest. A copse of trees greeted Oenghus on the other side of a shallow valley. He walked alongside the prince and princess of Kambe, leading his horse, while the heirs to the empire rode. He was eye level with the eight-year-old twins.

"Why do you wear a dress?" Sarabian asked.

Soataen chuckled at the question, his gaze resting softly on his daughter. The girl was striking, with the red hair of her mother and the blue eyes of her father. Beyond a doubt, she would grow into a beautiful woman, just as her mother had been. The late empress had died in childbirth, and Soataen had not taken another Oathbound.

"It's not a dress, your highness. It's a kilt," Oenghus

replied. His rumble was soft, like that of an amused bear. The child was not afraid, but then why should she be? The royal party was surrounded by a ring of the emperor's Hounds, two nursemaids, and a line of servants.

"It looks like a dress to me," the prince remarked. Aristarchus Jaal was as striking as his sister, but he had a sharp nose that, when he spoke, he already looked down.

"Maybe so," Oenghus shrugged, "but it keeps my legs free. I've a long stride, and——" He stuck his pipe between his lips and deftly untucked the long folds of wool from his belt, lifting the fabric up and over his head. "It makes for a cloak when it's cold. Pockets and all." He put his hands in the voluminous space at his sides to demonstrate. "Or you can dress up a bit." Another quick adjustment and he reached back, draping the loose ends over his shoulder and tying them together to create a respectable sash.

"That's hardly any better," Aristarchus drawled.

"I like it, Ari," Sarabian retorted. "Do Nuthaanian women wear kilts, too?" She wore a stiff riding outfit with voluminous split trousers that retained its appearance of a dress. No doubt freedom of movement appealed to the young girl.

Oenghus shrugged. "They wear whatever the Void they like." Both children's eyes went wide at his curse and he received a disapproving sound from their nursemaids. "In Nuthaan, our women rule and bloodlines are traced through mothers. Men have no place as clan chiefs."

"In Kambe," Aristarchus inserted, "those with the rightful blood rule."

"Aye, well, blood is thin, your highness. It spills easily in Nuthaan."

"A testimony to your own daughter's rule, Lord Saevaldr," Soataen remarked. "Chieftess Freyr has held the throne longer than any other."

Oenghus tugged on a braid. "Kari got her mother's mind and wisdom, and my stubbornness."

"And fierceness, no doubt."

"You don't much know Morigan," Oenghus grunted. "Don't get that woman angry."

Soataen chuckled. "I'll keep that in mind."

"Your nymph likes Morigan very much, Father," Aristarchus remarked.

Oenghus flinched at the possessive term. He looked away, out to the sea of green, before his eyes could betray his anger.

"The nymph is very skittish with all others," the emperor agreed.

"Including us," Aristarchus sniffed.

"Give it time," Soataen replied. "I once had a horse that was as wild as could be. It took patience and persistence, but eventually it responded to me. We Jaals are like a river, my son, the strongest rock will eventually give way to our will."

Oenghus was on the verge of snarling out a sharp rebuke, but Sarabian's focus was still on his kilt and the girl's enthusiasm stilled his tongue. "Father, can I wear a kilt?" the girl asked. Her face was so bright that it softened Oenghus' mood and reminded him of why he was here in Kambe. Oenghus felt a pang of memory for his own daughters—some grown, most dead. Denying them anything had always been a grueling ordeal.

"If you like, Sara," Soataen replied. Apparently, an

emperor was no different. "I'll have the tailors fit you for one." He nodded to the nursemaids who were riding behind. The nod was a silent command, a gesture that Oenghus had seen repeated many times. Soataen rarely issued direct orders. He simply spoke, nodded, and expected everyone surrounding him to take note and carry out his wishes. "What about you, Aristarchus?"

"I do not wear dresses," the boy said, raising his chin.

"Nuthaan and Kambe are close allies. Dress or no, you would do well to learn the customs of other lands, especially our allies."

The emperor had invited Oenghus on their weekly ride through the brisk countryside for just such a reason. Oenghus was not the typical Nuthaanian ambassador who came to the palace—he was not interested in court politics or pleasing royalty. Rather than being offended, the emperor found the berserker's blunt nature a refreshing change, akin to having a wild bear chained in the palace.

"I have, Father," Aristarchus protested and turned to Oenghus, "Is it true that berserkers feel no pain?"

"We feel it, "Oenghus grunted. "But we use it— same as channeling the Gift. In battle, a berserker is only half the fighter until he is wounded. When the blood begins to flow, he becomes stronger—until he drops dead."

Sarabian looked thoughtful as she reached forward to stroke her horse's neck. "Can women be berserkers?"

"Our women aren't foolish enough to risk the grog."

"Is that your Brimgrog there?" Aristarchus pointed to the flask on his belt. Oenghus nodded in reply and unconsciously touched the flask out of long habit. "May I see it?"

"You may not, lad."

Aristarchus bristled.

"It is sacred," Oenghus explained, holding the prince's gaze.

"I thought Nuthaanians did not worship the Guardians," Sarabian smoothly inserted, nudging her pristine horse between her brother and the berserker.

"We don't," Oenghus stated. "Only a fool would want to be worshipped. Respect, however, is an honor, and it is earned. But how can we respect someone we have not met, or for that matter, worship something we do not know?"

"You must know your flask very well then, sir." Amusement danced in the girl's eyes.

Oenghus barked a laugh. "Most Nuthaanians do, your highness."

The emperor beamed with approval at his daughter. She had deftly diffused tension with a well-chosen word, and accomplished it without prickling prince or guest.

"I have heard," Aristarchus drawled, "that berserkers cut down their allies."

"Aye, in the heat of battle," Oenghus confirmed. "But every veteran knows not to get near a berserker when he's drunk his grog."

"Hardly desirable allies," the prince smirked.

Oenghus bared his teeth. "We are the ones who go first. We soften the enemies for Kambe."

Aristarchus arched a brow. "That is what a cavalry is for."

"Berserkers run in front of the cavalry charge."

"Impossible," Aristarchus said, but there was more

disbelief than demand. "The horses would overrun you."

"Are you sure about that, your highness?"

Both heirs looked down, and then back up, taking in his height. "Lord Saevaldr *is* tall, Ari. But I doubt he could outrun Snow," Sarabian said, leaning forward to plant a kiss on the mare's neck.

"Would you indulge my children with a demonstration, Lord Saevaldr?" the emperor requested.

Oenghus chuckled, passing his reins to a guard. "Aye, your majesty. To the tree on that hill over there."

The Hounds shifted, the servants huffed, and Soataen looked at Oenghus in surprise. The emperor was not often challenged to a race. By the look in his eye, he was not displeased.

"At your leisure," Soataen said, bringing his horse to bear.

"If you'll count down, your highness," Oenghus nodded to Sarabian as he adjusted the folds of his kilt, unslung his targe and slipped his arm through the straps, taking up his war hammer in the same hand so the haft wouldn't tangle in his legs.

Sarabian beamed, and began the count, starting at ten with an air of breathless anticipation. "Three, two, one—Go!" In the heartbeat between words, the young princess dug in her heels. Both men started in surprise when Sarabian bolted ahead. Soataen's amusement vanished as he urged his steed into action at the same time Oenghus surged forward.

Snow was a blur of white and the princess clung to the mare's back as rider and horse flowed through green grass like a white sail over the sea.

Oenghus caught up to the horse at the basin. Snow

took one look at the giant racing alongside and her eye rolled with panic. She veered sharply to the side, colliding with the emperor's steed. Snow tripped, sending the emperor's horse dancing to the side with a stumble.

As Snow went down, Oenghus dove for the child, knocking her off the rolling horse's back. Equine and human screams filled his ears. A heavy weight rolled onto to his leg, and then a hoof bit into his calf as the horse staggered upright.

Dust and grass clouded his vision. Blinded, he scrambled towards the screaming child. When his vision cleared, he saw the princess laying on her back, clutching at her leg. A dark spot grew like ink on her riding dress.

Soataen leapt from his horse and rushed to his daughter's side the same instant that Oenghus reached her.

"Sarabian, look at me," the emperor ordered, taking her face in his hands. Oenghus drew his blade, slicing the voluminous fabric in search of the wound. A splintered bone protruded from her shin. Soataen clenched his jaw and looked away, swallowing a pained sound. The emperor focused on his daughter, holding her gaze with his own, speaking firmly. "You are all right, everything is going to be fine." And on and on he reassured as Oenghus examined the fracture.

"I can heal this," Oenghus assured them both, but inwardly he grimaced at the puncture wound and the age of the child. He shoved the thought aside. Kindness would not help her now. "But it'll need leather, Soataen."

The lack of title went unnoticed as the two men

locked eyes. Soataen nodded, and unthreaded his belt as the rest of the company arrived. Aristarchus raced to his sister's side, but Soataen ordered the boy back.

"Now then, your highness," Oenghus said, entering her line of sight. He bared his teeth, white against the black of his beard. "You will become a berserker today, and afterwards you'll be stronger for it." The young girl looked at him through a veil of tears and snot and gasping breath. "I want you to bite down on this bit of leather," he said evenly. There was nothing worse than a soft voice when one was in agony. "I'm going to pour my Brimgrog onto your leg. It's a bit bent is all, and the wound needs cleaning—don't look at it," he said firmly while her father pinned her to the ground. "Brimgrog is sacred, so it'll burn. I want you to use that burn, Sarabian. I want you to channel it to strike fear into your enemies."

"I don't have any enemies," she whimpered.

"Blackness is your enemy. You look at the sky and you keep it blue." It was an order, the same he had given to hardened warriors on a battlefield. During a healing, the wounded fared better if they were conscious.

Oenghus nodded to Soataen, who placed the belt between his daughter's teeth. As soon as the child bit down, Oenghus uncorked his flask, pinned her leg and poured the Brimgrog into the wound. Sarabian arched, screaming with desperation. While the princess was in the thrall of agony, Oenghus gripped the small leg and forced the bone back beneath the skin, holding it in place like a clamp.

When the burn dissipated, the girl's eyes were rolling, but she was awake. He grunted with approval, and placed his free hand over her forehead, summoning the Lore. Oenghus waded into the currents of Life, seeking out Sarabian's ruined flesh and taking her pain upon himself.

The Sylph's bond was always with him in one way or another; the connection was as enduring as their spirits. Yasine held the essence of Life itself, the very source of the Gift, which was why Oenghus, a crazed berserker, found it so easy to heal. In minutes, he could heal wounds that would take the most talented of their Order days, or even weeks. Sharing a bond with the Goddess of All had its advantages.

When he withdrew his awareness, Sarabian was asleep, her features calm with rest. The emperor looked from his peaceful daughter, to her leg where the flesh was whole.

"It's healed!" Aristarchus shouted in disbelief.

"Only a bruise," Soataen breathed, looking at the Nuthaaninan.

"Aye," Oenghus sat back, tugging his beard. "Helps the mind heal actually. Otherwise, the mind tends to latch onto the last flare of pain. The bruising is sort of a symbolic healing."

"You saved her—" Emotion caught Soataen's throat and he quickly removed his cloak and bundled his daughter up.

"Just quicker than most."

"The horse rolled," Soataen continued, lifting his daughter in his arms. "She would have been crushed."

"I do what I can for anyone who needs it," Oenghus replied.

Soataen nodded his gratitude, a slight dip of his chin that held the weight of an empire behind it.

"You should not have raced in the first place," Aristarchus argued. The boy was near to tears.

"All choices have consequences, Aristarchus," Soataen said. "The choice not to race, the choice to stand aside, the choice to simply watch."

Oenghus stood, following the emperor's gaze to the white horse. Snow held her right foreleg off the ground, standing on three, huffing with pain.

"It was Sarabian's decision to enter the race without council, and it was Snow who threw her. It will not happen again." Soataen nodded to one of his nearby Hounds. The same gesture that assumed everyone within range was keenly aware of the emperor's slightest thought, so much so that a nod would communicate his will.

The guard drew a curved blade and stepped forward. It took Oenghus a moment to realize what that nod had meant. He blinked in surprise and stepped forward, planting himself between executioner and horse. "I can heal the horse," he said quickly, holding up a hand. "She'll just have to limp back, and I'll have her good as new in the stables."

Soataen's gaze turned hard and cold as granite. "I thank you, Lord Saevaldr, but my order stands."

"Snow was just startled is all. Takes a trained warhorse to become accustomed to a berserker in full run." Oenghus placed a careful hand on the mare, stroking her gently.

"I understand and respect Nuthaanian customs, but here, in Kambe, my word is Law. Step aside," the emperor ordered with quiet power.

"Your daughter loves this horse, your majesty. It's plain, even to me," Oenghus pressed.

"Please, Father, listen to him," Aristarchus pleaded.

"Sarabian must learn a hard lesson today—that every action, every choice leads somewhere, good or ill. She entered our contest without consultation, without plan."

"As children often do," Oenghus argued.

"She is not a child; she is the heir of Kambe," there was no softness in the emperor's voice. "Do not press me, Lord Saevaldr. I am a patient man, but when I have decided upon a course of action, I will not hear argument. I am not a man who tolerates disobedience."

Oenghus frowned, lowering his hand to the prince's shoulder. He nudged the boy a step back. The Hound advanced, gripped Snow's bridle and jerked her neck up, slashing her throat. Bright blood gushed from the jugular, staining her pristine coat. The horse thrashed and slowly weakened, kneeling and finally falling as the life flowed from her body, pooling in the grass around Oenghus' boots.

The emperor turned with his daughter in his arms, and then paused, glancing over his shoulder. "Thank you again, Lord Saevaldr. As a father, I'm sure you understand."

Oenghus looked down at the young prince. Tears streamed down his cheeks as he watched the final death throes of his sister's beloved horse. Oenghus squeezed the boy's shoulder.

No, he did not understand. Not one bit.

BLIGHT

TIME SLIPPED LIKE sand through his fingertips when he wanted nothing more than to hold on to every last grain. But Time was fickle. Every night, the Sylph came, slipping through moonlight, falling into his arms.

During the day, Oenghus occupied himself with his court duties, learning, what was to him a tedious and complicated new dance. He might be an uncivilized barbarian, but that did not mean he could not adapt; however, it did mean he had little patience for it.

Whitemount was not unlike the Wise Ones Isle. But even during his apprenticeship with Marsais, Oenghus had spent as little time as possible inside his Order's castle. When he visited the Isle, he preferred to find rooms in the town. And whenever possible, to keep his sanity, that is precisely what he did in Whitemount.

He left the organization of the infirmaries to Morigan, and lent his healing talents wherever they were needed. Whitemount was not a backwater town. The city boasted many talented healers, but none were as gifted as the Nuthaanian pair. For the first time in twelve years, Oenghus began to brew potions. This was a time-consuming process, one unsuited for the battlefields. Oenghus had missed the challenges brewing brought.

Unfortunately, it gave him time to think, and although the emperor had been nothing but a gentleman with Yasine, Oenghus continued to be ill at ease. As with anyone who wielded power, there were dark facets to the man.

Weeks turned into months. Winter flowed into spring, and the rains began to interfere with Yasine's nightly visits. For two nights, the rains kept her away, and on the third, a knock interrupted his mixing.

"Come."

The door opened, and he turned to find a harried page. "Lord Saevaldr—Wise One." No one seemed to know what title to use for the unconventional healer. "Your presence is urgently required in the south. There has been a fever outbreak."

"Spotted fever?"

The page shook his head. "That is what they first thought, m'lord, but now the healers fear Blight."

"Blight in Kambe?" he barked.

"Yes, m'lord. His Majesty has asked his royal healers to assist."

"I take it Morigan has been told?" The page nodded. "Tell her I'll meet her in the stables."

As the page scurried to deliver his message, Oenghus gathered supplies in his rucksack, strapped on his belt, shouldered his targe, and hooked his hammer into place. Blight spread quickly.

At the doorway he stopped, took a last look at the wind-battered balcony, touched his sacred flask, and went out into the storm.

"How the Void did you let this get out of hand!" Oenghus bellowed at a healer, who was soaked to the bone and shivering in the night. The soldiers who stood guard on the other side of the barricades took their eyes off the besieged district and looked warily at the enraged berserker. Inquisitor Ashe's presence was not helping Oenghus' mood. The district was a day's fast ride from the palace, a major trading port in Wyrim's Fist, and home to a large Chapterhouse of the Blessed Order. After handing over the nymph, Ashe had taken up residence there.

On Ashe's orders, a barricade had been erected around the entire quarter, trapping the healthy and sick in with the Blighted.

Well used to Oenghus' bellow, Morigan ignored her kinsman. Her eyes were on the city and the main road, which was utterly devoid of lamplight and people.

"We thought it was the Spotted Fever," the shivering Kamberian healer defended. "All the symptoms were present."

"We quarantined the infected," an older, bent woman added.

"But it was Blight," Oenghus grunted.

"They came out of the graves on the very night the fever victims died—there were so many of them," the shivering healer said, wiping water from his eyes. "The district was overrun before sunrise."

"We were battling the Blighted, getting the healthy out—" the Captain of the Watch added, looking at Ashe. "The honorable Inquisitor ordered us to erect a barrier. Some of my men are still in there."

Oenghus could have guessed that much. He eyed the makeshift barrier: wagons, timber, and some stone on the main roads, but mostly wards. The Wise One who had set the wards had fled immediately after. Wise Ones were not known for their helpfulness, but rather, they were known for the high prices they charged for their valuable skills.

"I will not risk innocent lives," Ashe stated. "Anyone who steps foot beyond this barrier is considered infected. As soon as the rain stops, we will put it to the torch."

Before Oenghus could bellow his reply, a shadow darted from a doorway at the end of the road. As it neared, it took shape: a cloaked figure was running towards the barricade. A flash of eyes, a sound, the way the figure hunched over—Oenghus reacted. As the guards drew back their arrows, he vaulted over the barricade, crashing through the wards with a burst of energy. Lightning pounded into his back, grasping at his legs. It tickled.

The archers hesitated.

"Shoot!" Ashe ordered.

Arrows were loosed, Oenghus reached the cloaked figure, put his arm around the woman and her babe, and raised his shield, catching a barrage of arrows. He roared at the soldiers, shaking the surrounding buildings with fury.

The soldiers, the Inquisitor, and the healers were all

staring forward—except Morigan who reacted as quickly as Oenghus. She stepped behind the Inquisitor and shoved the woman through the broken barrier. The surprising strength behind the shove toppled the armored warrior, sending her sprawling into the mud.

"Oh, dear," Morigan said, planting herself in front of the breach. "It looks like you've caught Blight, Inquisitor. By your own orders, these men should kill you."

"You pushed me," the Inquisitor stood, wiping the mud off her golden tunic.

"The commotion startled me, I tripped," Morigan smiled, and clapped her hands to get everyone's attention. "Now then, listen up. The first rule of fighting the Blight is not to create more bodies to infect. You can either keep listening to the Inquisitor, in which case you will be obligated to kill her, or you can follow my instructions." All ears were listening to the confident healer. "I need soldiers to guard the infirmaries, a squad to fight the Blighted, and as many healers as you can muster."

"That's madness," Ashe said.

"Then we can do it your way," Morigan said, putting her hands on her hips.

The soldiers' attention was pried from the standoff to the end of the road, where swift shadows emerged out of the darkness. Bows were drawn back, but the berserker met the walking dead with hammer in hand. The first boil-ridden, rotting foe fell like wheat beneath a scythe. The second lost its head on the backward swing. And after that, Oenghus found his rhythm. The shadows fell one after another, until the final was pounded into a shapeless mass by his shield.

But this group of Blighted was immature. The longer the Blight festered, the stronger the mutations.

The Captain of the Watch did not need anymore convincing. He began issuing orders. Satisfied, Morigan stepped through the barrier, and joined Oenghus. She took the terrified woman and squalling child under her arm.

"I like it when you get all pushy," he bared his teeth.

"And I hate resorting to it," she sighed, checking over the mother and child for wounds.

"Hopefully, none of these things have had time to grow."

"Aye," Morigan nodded in agreement. "You start the clearing and I'll start the tending."

Oenghus knocked his hammer against his targe, dislodging a rope of clinging entrails. He looked to the barricade and shouted, "Bring oil! And you healers, get your arses in here, or I'll drag you in!"

MOANS AND FEVERED rumblings filled the infirmary. Unlike most of the makeshift wards that had sprung up in the district, this one was permanent: a temple of Chaim. Here, the clerics refused to abandon the people when others of their Order had fled the district. If Inquisitor Ashe had carried out her plan, she would have burnt members of her own Order.

The healers fought a battle on both fronts. The sickness that had been brought on a merchant ship was both Spotted fever and the Blight, all wrapped in a nasty bundle.

Oenghus lifted a boy's head, and pressed an elixir to his lips. "Drink up, lad," he murmured. The dry, cracked lips parted, and the boy took a sip. Oenghus had never seen such an aggressive mix. The spots of the fever had turned to Blight boils in a matter of days. If not for Morigan's talents, they would all have become infected. Her elixirs were legendary. Three days had passed, and the worst was over—the plague contained, fizzling out through brute force, quarantine, body disposal, but mostly, Morigan's supreme organization.

Oenghus and Morigan made a good pair—they always had. He glanced over to the next cot, where she was bending over a patient. Morigan met his gaze and smiled. Dark circles ringed her eyes, but the lines of worry had left.

"The emperor won't want to part with you," he said.

"I'll do what I always do," she chuckled, "I'll tell him it was all you."

Oenghus glared at her. Praise led to official positions, which inevitably led to court workings, clan maneuverings, and the dreaded mire of politics. But for Morigan, he would shoulder the responsibility, just as she had abandoned her homeland to watch his back.

When the boy had sipped the elixir to the last drop, Oenghus eyed his patient critically. The boy's fever was gone, the Blight boils mere black marks on the skin, but the lad's color was worrisome. It was grey, and the boy was weak, hovering so very close to death.

Without a thought to his own exhaustion, Oenghus slipped one hand over the boy's stomach and the other over his forehead, binding himself to spirit and body. The Lore was a soft murmur on his lips as he waded into the currents of the Gift, searching the boy with his mind's eye. The boy's spirit was as grey as his skin, and Oenghus bolstered his patient with his own strength.

Healing required sacrifice, and Oenghus had never turned his back on an innocent—no matter how tired he was. When the spirit responded with a glow of dim light, he carefully withdrew, pulling his awareness back along an ethereal tether to his own body. He shook away disorientation as if ridding himself of a cloak and reached for a rag in a bucket, squeezing out the excess water and mopping the boy's brow.

Another spirit stirred within, a ripple of fear. Oenghus froze. His awareness turned inward, searching, reaching towards the bond that he shared with the Sylph. Yasine had been content these last days, touching lightly on his spirit everyday; a caressing greeting that he would return so she knew all was well. But the touch had changed.

Fear turned to panic, a surge that sped to his heart like a scream. Pain jarred him, made all the worse because it was not his own.

"Oen?" Morigan's voice brought him around.

"Something's wrong," he said, hoarsely. A pit was opening in his stomach and he felt himself falling. "I need to go."

Morigan grabbed his arm with an iron grip. "What's wrong?"

"The *nymph*," he stressed the word.

"I'll be there as soon as I can. Scrub yourself good and thorough or you'll bring this plague to the palace."

He nodded.

As usual, Morigan was right, but every moment he spent scrubbing the foul smelling concoction on his body felt like an eternity wasted. Panic and pain traveled through their bond, until all was silent. He rode north like a storm, and on the long road to Whitemount, silence turned to rage—a chill that made him shiver.

13

RIGHT OF VENGEANCE

OENGHUS RODE THROUGH the night and all through the day, only stopping when his mount was on the verge of collapse. He used his title to demand a messengers' exchange, and continued the swift ride. When he rode through the palace gates, a groom stepped forward to take the reins of his laboring horse. As soon as Oenghus' boots touched the stone, a plump, greying man who had all the makings of a finicky cat, hurried across the courtyard. Oenghus recognized him as the Steward.

"Lord Saevaldr," there was a hint of relief in the Steward's imperious tone. "I've just dispatched a messenger for you. His majesty requires your immediate presence."

Oenghus nearly asked after the nymph, but caught himself. Any questions would raise suspicion; instead, he asked after the emperor.

"If you will follow me."

In the months since Oenghus' arrival, after healing the princess, he had earned the emperor's trust, becoming an unofficial advisor of sorts. And gradually, despite the incident involving Sarabian's horse, Oenghus had come to respect Soataen as a man. Whatever had happened to Yasine, the emperor would inform him.

Soataen's personal chambers were not extravagant, but well lived-in, with protective wards covering every inch of wall space. Soataen huddled in a worn armchair, close to a fireplace that reminded Oenghus of a giant maw. The emperor was pale—shivering beneath a heavy fur blanket. At first, Oenghus feared fever, but there were no spots, no boils, and no sheen to his skin.

"Leave us."

The steward bowed and left, as did the emperor's personal healer. The Hounds, however, remained, ever watchful, ever on guard, as alert as the animals they were named for.

The door closed, and Oenghus walked to the fireplace, eyeing Soataen from the side. The ruler's sharp eyes were faded, turned inward, as if searching his memories.

"You appear ill, your majesty," Oenghus said, hoping to speed things along. The chill radiating along Yasine's bond was like a shield. He could not reach out to her.

"I only just dispatched a message. How is it that you arrived so quickly?" Soataen did not look at the Wise One.

"I came back to Whitemount for supplies," he lied.

"How goes the outbreak in the south?"

"Contained," Oenghus reported. "Morigan mixed an elixir that targeted both Blight and the fever. It worked. The Blessed Order would have burnt the district to the ground."

"Precisely why I value my Nuthaanian allies—for their loyalty and resourcefulness. Sometimes," Soataen murmured, "I fear we rely too heavily on our gods." The words were heresy, as far as the Order was concerned, but Oenghus' kin felt the same. The emperor's blue eyes flickered to the towering Nuthaanian. "I have a request. It requires your word."

"I do not give my word without knowing the task," Oenghus rumbled.

"Your discretion as a healer, then."

"Has something happened, your majesty?" he asked, trying to keep the impatience out of his words. Patience had never been a strong point. He tightened his fist to keep his words in check and tried again to reach out to Yasine through their bond. This time, she responded. The icy shield melted, and she reached back, brushing his spirit. There was grief in her touch.

"My nymph is not well," the emperor murmured, turning his gaze to the fireplace. Oenghus' heart lurched. He wanted to shake the answer loose from the pale man. "When my healer, or anyone approaches, she —becomes distressed." A muscle twitched in the emperor's jaw. And every word brought Oenghus closer to understanding. The fear, the panic, the pain—the berserker stepped forward, flexing his fists. But Yasine frantically reached out to him through their bond, silently pleading for control. He stopped himself.

"I trust you, Oenghus," the emperor continued, too lost in his own misery to notice the looming Nuthaanian. "See if you can heal my nymph—she trusted you in Northolt and I think she will trust you now. Speak of this to no one."

"Aye," Oenghus could not keep the disgust out of his voice.

Soataen did not look at him, but kept his eyes purposefully ahead. "Leave and come back to me when she is healed."

Oenghus vibrated with restraint. "Yes, your majesty," he said through clenched teeth. It took all his considerable will to turn his back on the coward and force his feet to move. Without a backward glance, Oenghus strode from the chambers. A Hound broke off, escorting him to the rooms at the other end of the wing —where the empress had once lived.

Two women guards flanked the arch. Both of them frowned at the Nuthaanian. Without a word, Oenghus was given over to one of the guards. The Hound waited outside while the woman showed him into the wing.

"The nymph is in her garden," the guard said. "When anyone enters—she grows agitated."

"I wonder why," he growled, scanning the trio of fretting attendants who stood by an open doorway, gazing out into the night.

"Bring her here," the guard ordered the attendants. They paled as one. And Oenghus looked out the elegant doors to the garden beyond. It was wild and overgrown.

"There's no need," he said, stepping onto the balcony.

"I cannot allow——" the guard began.

He cut her off. "The emperor asked me to heal his nymph without causing her distress. She knows me. I'll not have to hack my way through that." He gestured at the thorns and briars. Still, the guard looked hesitant. "Do you want me to go bother his majesty, and ask him to give me my orders again in your presence?"

The guard's eyes flickered from the shelter of warmth to the threatening foliage. "I'll wait here."

Oenghus grunted and walked down the steps into the garden. As far as cages went, hers was spacious. The garden walls were high and mysterious and Yasine's mere presence made the foliage thrive.

In a matter of months, a single glimpse of the nymph in the throne room had become legend. Yasine's arrival ignited a wild fire of imagination, spawning a deluge of romantic drivel from every harper in the kingdom.

But in Oenghus' experience, romance was for fools. Love had nothing to do with flowery speeches or wooing flattery. Love was in the simple things—the every day. In a laugh, a smile, and most especially, tears.

The foliage folded back as he approached. And he eyed the splinters in a few branches, as if someone had hacked his way through. Oenghus let his bond pull him towards the Sylph. She sat under a wide oak, watching the rain dance on a nearby pond.

"The fool," she said without turning.

Her voice was like a glacier and he stopped in his tracks. A fine wool cloak hung loosely around her shoulders, exposing part of her mark. The sprawling oak tree was vibrant in the dark. He could trace its branches and leaves by memory, could feel its same pattern spiraling around his spine. Still intact, through death and beyond, and other men—the Sylph's bond was as eternal as their love.

"Soataen forced himself on you," Oenghus broke the chill.

She turned. Dew misted her eyes, but no tears fell. "I planned to go willingly to his bed, very soon, but he grew impatient. When I fled, he sent his Hounds after me. They hacked their way through my garden." Yasine sprang to her feet, radiating power and anger. "He didn't even have the bollocks to run me down himself."

Shadows caressed her skin, as dark and cold as her heart, but beneath the frost, he sensed pain. Oenghus stepped forward, reaching for her. She flinched, and he paused. Slowing his movements, he gently cupped her chin, eyeing her injuries. There were bruises on her face and she held her arm close to her body.

"I'll kill the bastard," he growled.

Yasine looked him in the eye. "Do not interfere."

"I never swore."

"It is *my* right, Oenghus," she snapped, taking a step back. "By your own Nuthaanian law—vengeance is mine. And I swear mine will be far slower and more painful than any brutish attack you could inflict. I may not be able to use my power directly in this realm, but Soataen entered mine when he invaded my body. Everything he inflicted upon me, I shall return upon him a hundred-fold."

"What if he comes again?"

"He will not," she said coolly. "He'll find his manhood as flaccid as a dead fish."

There was something in her tone that reminded him of a spider that devoured its mate after a coupling. He was fully aware of the Goddess in front of him—the immense power coursing through her veins, the essence of all Life, above shame, or even pain.

"You could have stopped him, used your power—"

A tilt of her brow stopped his tongue.

"I could have, yes," she said. "And ruined my guise as a nymph, earned the Void's attention, and put the lives of everyone in this city at risk—to say nothing of the realms."

Oenghus frowned down at the Sylph. She was not without physical prowess.

Yasine sensed the errant thought. "I wanted to see how far he would go, what an innocent truly meant to him—not the facade he puts on when people are watching. I am disappointed with Soataen," she said simply. With that, the matter was closed.

Moving slowly, he opened her cloak and drew out her arm. Her wrist was swollen and bruised and bent at an odd angle. And suddenly, at his touch, all that power and strength sought comfort, and she gave herself over to his arms. He wrapped her in an embrace, cradling her head to his chest.

"You have never disappointed me, my rock," she whispered into his shirtfront.

"I'm bound to, one day," he said gruffly.

"You always say that." Tears slipped down her cheeks, mirroring his own pain. With Oenghus, for him alone, she let her walls down—for what was power without compassion, and what was wisdom without grief?

When Yasine pulled away, she settled herself in a cradle of roots, and he knelt at her side on the damp earth. "Soataen asked me to return after I heal you."

She nodded. "Heal him—it will do no good."

Oenghus tugged on his beard. Suddenly weary and drawn, she touched his arm, cooling his fury. "Please, my love," she whispered. "Spend these remaining months with me in peace." She led his hand to her stomach and he spread his fingers over warmth.

"When?" he asked in realization.

"Weeks ago, I think, before the rains. She is yours, and was not harmed." Yasine closed her eyes. "I can feel her already—a spark of life that will rage over this realm."

Oenghus placed his free hand over her forehead. The Lore was on the tip of his tongue when she spoke, "Swear to me."

She opened her eyes to his.

"I'll come back when I am done."

Yasine smiled. "I should like that."

He murmured the Lore, tied himself to shore and waded into the currents of Life, into the very same power that coursed through Yasine's veins. But where the Gift was a river, she was the sky and the sun and its endless source. He dared not stray close to her spirit. Instead, Oenghus directed his awareness straight to her bone, to the cuts and bruises marring her flesh. The injuries pained him, not for their severity, but because of his love. His concentration tottered, battling with grief and rage, until he gently peeked into her womb.

The child was like none that he had ever glimpsed: a roiling flame. Startled, Oenghus retreated, pulling himself back along the thin tether that tied his awareness to body. The currents tugged on him, but he persisted, focusing on shore until it released its hold. Oenghus blinked away the disorientation and shook himself, dislodging his unease.

Yasine was asleep. He smoothed back her hair, but kept his hand on her stomach, expecting heat, or a glow —something that would betray the child within. But all was normal.

Had they spawned a fire elemental?

Oenghus frowned at the thought. He tucked the

cloak firmly around her, and watched as the roots grew and shifted, creating a protective cocoon around the Sylph.

Before leaving, he touched the oak tree. "Watch her, old ones," he murmured, and instantly felt foolish. Marsais talked to trees, not him. With a final glance, he left to find the emperor and steeled himself to face the man who had just raped the love of all his lives.

THE EMPEROR SAT in front of the fireplace where Oenghus had left him, hunched and shivering like a man caught in the Keening. Oenghus wanted to pummel the man. He wanted to beat him into a squishy pulp and render his bones to dust. But Yasine had right of vengeance. And in Nuthaan, to ignore a woman's choice was to demean her, a crime as despicable as the rape itself. The berserker kept his body in check, but not his voice.

"She's with child," Oenghus announced without preamble.

Soataen's eyes sharped on the Nuthaanian. "You can tell so soon?"

"Aye—I can tell a lot of things." He let the words linger in the room.

With effort, Soataen straightened. "You gave your word. She is, after all, a nymph."

"I said nothing, your majesty," he growled. "But I

suggest, for your health, that you stay away from the nymph."

"Is that a threat?"

"I'm a healer. It's advice."

The emperor closed his mouth, gripped the armrests, and pushed himself to his feet. He swayed, and grabbed the mantel to steady himself. "Can you heal me?"

"I can try," Oenghus said. "What ails you?"

Soataen shifted. Color spread across his high cheekbones. "I have heard of a nymph's bond, but—" he faltered, glanced at his Hounds, and beckoned the giant closer. Oenghus loomed over the emperor as he watched the man's shaking hands. Soataen untied his robe, revealing a smooth, muscled torso, and then his fingers dropped to his trousers. The laces fell and Soataen looked away, unable to stand the sight.

Oenghus looked down. A mark of thorns wound around the emperor's shaft.

"What has she done to me?" Soataen asked in a thin, tremulous whisper.

Oenghus scratched his beard. "Didn't you know? That's the way of nymphs, your majesty. You got what you gave."

"But the legends?" Soataen rasped. Fear filled his eyes and Oenghus relished it.

"Do you believe every legend about yourself? How much truth is in those?"

"How do I get rid of it?" Soataen snapped.

Oenghus bit back a suggestion of an axe. "I've seen a lot of strange things in the brothels, but nothing like this." Oenghus thought the emperor might faint. He had no intention of catching him, so he pressed on, "A healing *might* help. But I think, what matters most, is the nymph's comfort. Treat her well and maybe you'll feel better."

"Of course," Soataen said, looking as though he'd be sick.

"On the bed, your majesty."

Eager to be free of the mark of thorns, Soataen obeyed, settling himself on his bed. Oenghus tried not to think about this bed, of what the coward had likely done here, in this very room.

Oenghus placed one hand on Soataen's stomach and the other on his forehead. To say he was not tempted to snap the emperor's neck would be an understatement, but Yasine's plea echoed in his ears: would he give her months of peace, would he honor her choice, or follow his own rage?

If Oenghus Saevaldr had learned one thing from his old master Marsais, it was the value of manipulation and blackmail. While the Nuthaanian usually had no stomach for underhanded tactics, he employed them now, "There is one other thing, your majesty."

"Anything."

"Allow me access to your nymph's garden day and night."

Soataen's eyes narrowed. "What are you suggesting?"

"That you keep your nymph happy."

The emperor looked into the steady gaze of his only hope. Soataen closed his eyes, and breathed, "Granted. I don't want to see her again."

"Very wise of you, your majesty," Oenghus murmured.

Nymphs and men bonded, but whereas nymphs had

no control over the connection, the Sylph shaped it to her will. As Oenghus plunged inside of the emperor, he saw the poison, the pain, and the shame—a mirror of the betrayal reflected back on the emperor.

Oenghus did not even try to ease Soataen's suffering.

14

ONLY A HOPE

AS THE DAYS passed, the emperor regained his strength and returned to his duties as if nothing had occurred. Spring turned to summer, and Oenghus spent long days with Yasine, and longer nights.

During the days, they walked in her garden where she grew exotic plants and flowers for his brewing. And together, they worked and refined, unlocking secrets in his workshop. Yasine taught Morigan as well, gifting the healer with her knowledge of plants.

The days were peaceful and easy, and all the while her belly grew. Summer turned the trees gold and autumn bowed to winter, until life emerged with gentle rains.

A soft patter mingled with the pop of flame. The room glowed with warmth in the wet night. Yasine lay on her side, moulding to his body, savoring his heat. Oenghus' arms encircled her; one hand rested on a full breast, round with pregnancy, and the other on her swollen belly.

Oenghus smiled into her hair as the child pressed a

foot against its womb. Such a small foot, smaller than his thumb. He traced its outline, and then ran his fingers lightly over the heel, tickling. The foot withdrew, and he waited. When the foot returned, he tickled, and again, it withdrew, coming back faster, trying to stretch. Oenghus poked back and the tiny foot pressed hard against his finger. And then like a drum beat, his child pounded against his fingertip, kicking.

Yasine moaned and shifted, rolled onto her back, found that uncomfortable, and rolled towards her bedmate. "I'd forgotten how miserable this part is." Oenghus wrapped her in his arms and rubbed the small of her back. "Hmm, that nearly makes it tolerable."

The infant kicked against Oenghus' gut.

"You'll be able to play with your father soon," she murmured.

Oenghus' hand stilled for a moment. When he moved again, it was to tighten his hold on the Sylph. He did not want to exchange the mother for the child—he did not want to lose her. Despite the fire, the warm furs and blankets, the room turned cold.

"I'll be with you," Yasine whispered, pulling back to meet his eye. "Our bond is as eternal as our spirits."

"Not the same," he croaked.

Yasine ran her fingers through his unruly hair. "I am restless. It's not just this child. I want to walk my realms, stretch my mind."

"I know." He could not find the words, but he sensed her growing disquiet. A walled garden was hardly suitable for a Goddess.

"She will need you. Protect her, let her grow."

"I'll do my best."

The Goddess of All smiled, sadly. A tear slipped down her cheek. "So much depends upon her."

His eyes narrowed. "I thought you said there was no vision?"

"Only a hope. A spark in the darkness." There was fear in her voice. And Oenghus realized that she was holding something back: she did not know if they would be reunited.

His eyes flickered down to her belly, as if he could peer into the womb that held the tiny spirit of flame. As if the child sensed his gaze, Yasine's belly hardened, contracting with a cramp of pain, and a tremor. Yasine closed her eyes. It had begun.

When the contraction released its hold, Oenghus cupped her face. "I don't want to let you go."

"And I don't want to be let go," she admitted. "I will need your strength, my love." He kissed her lips, and her tears mingled with their breaths, tasting of grief. "I must go to my garden."

It took effort to release her, to stand and help her find her feet. Every moment felt as if it would be their last. Another contraction gave her pause and he rubbed her back as she rode it out.

"An attendant will summon you," she said.

"Aye."

"Bring Morigan."

Again he nodded, and she stepped into the moonlight.

15

THE SPARK

7th of Greentide, 1994 A.S.

THE HOURS PASSED, one after another, like a slow march towards death. Each step grew with intensity, and Oenghus was powerless to halt the pangs of birth and the inevitable conclusion.

Yasine did not need either healer. But he stayed with her as she paced her garden, back and forth, with the restlessness of something wild. When her body was ready, she squatted by her pond, gripping roots for support.

The Sylph barely made a noise, until the final push. But it was not a grunt nor a cry—it was a chant, a quiet, breathless song in a language both familiar and foreign, the language of trees and earth and all that lived. It was like a breath, and with a gasp, the infant slipped free.

Oenghus caught the child in one large hand, expecting to be burnt, but the tiny infant was flesh and blood and as slippery as every child he had ever delivered. His daughter's first cry was like the tremulous note of a bird finding its song. But he took little pleasure in the new life when another was at its end.

Yasine fell to the ground and curled in the moss, still chanting as she fought for breath. She began to glow with warmth, filling the dark garden with light.

"Yasine—" he began, but the glow intensified and gathered, pulsing along the cord, filling the tiny infant that lay cradled in his hand. As warmth entered the child, color drained from the mother—all the life flowed into her daughter until the Sylph was worn and pale beyond words.

The light flared, the infant sneezed, and a puff of flame burst from her drooping ears. The child began to cry as the light faded.

Morigan reined in her surprise, and moved to deliver the placenta before wrapping Yasine in a blanket.

"Yasine," he called her name, as he felt the life draining from her. The mark on his back was fading, until she finally clung to this realm by a single thread. There was no strength left in her.

Morigan checked for bleeding, put a hand on the Sylph's forehead, noting her temperature, and then found her erratic pulse "I don't know what's wrong, but she needs bolstering, Oen."

Panic clutched at Oenghus' heart. He could stop her death, bolster her spirit with his own, but one look from Yasine stilled him. With her eyes, she pleaded.

"Oenghus," Morigan said, firmly.

"It's my will, Morigan," the Sylph breathed. The words nearly broke him. And realization paled the kindly healer. "Watch him for me, please."

"I had a mind to already," Morigan replied.

"I know," she smiled. "Let me hold my daughter."

Oenghus propped Yasine up, and pressed the child to her breast. His daughter stopped her squalling and suckled eagerly.

The Sylph smiled down at her daughter. "Isiilde," she whispered and looked at Oenghus for his opinion.

"A fine name," he croaked, struggling with choice, even as Yasine struggled with breath.

"Please," she begged. "Let me go."

"You don't ask much."

"Only from you." Yasine paused to swallow. It seemed a great effort. "Let her find her own path."

"I'll be a father to her—as with any other child."

The Sylph closed her eyes, and did not speak again. Slowly, the mark ebbed on his back and he felt her spirit growing distant as her body grew cold, until it was nothing but a shell. Oenghus buried his nose in her hair, aching to join his Sylph.

A touch finally pierced the emptiness in his heart.

"Oen," Morigan said. "The babe will get cold."

He nodded and gently removed Yasine's arms from her child, and took his daughter in hand. All was blurry. He sniffed and wiped his eyes with a brisk hand. His vision cleared. Bright emerald eyes met his, wide and curious, and full of life.

Oenghus poked her tiny foot and she pushed against his fingertip. "I swear," he said to his daughter.

If you enjoyed *Untold Tales*, and would like to see more
of Isiilde and Marsais, please consider leaving a review.
Reviews help authors keep writing.

Keep up to date with the latest news, releases, and
giveaways.
It's quick and easy and spam free.
Sign up at www.sabrinaflynn.com/news

APPENDIX

Acacia Mael (ah·kay·shaa may·el) - Knight Captain of the Blessed Order on the Isle of the Wise Ones.

Afarim - Winged race of the Isle of Winds

Ardmoor - Void-worshipping barbarians in Vaylin.

Asmara - A Guardian of Iilenshar, or the Guardian of Love, also known as the Everchild. Asmara was six when the Orb shattered, and has not aged a day since. Daughter of Zahra, sister of Chaim.

Assumer - A race that can assume any shape.

Auroch - A massive bull-type creature found in Nuthaan and the Fell Wastes

Bastardlands - The continent that lies between the west and east. Separated by two chasms on either side, it's believed that the Keeper erected the Gates (chasms) to trap the Guardians of Morchaint.

Berserker's Rite - Some Nuthaanian warriors risk drinking Brimgrog on the eve of the Reddened Month. Most warriors die. The ones who survive have a reputation for being volatile and lethal.

Blessed Order - An Order that worships the Guardians of Iilenshar.

Blood Moon - A day and a night of light. All three moons are visible in the summer sky. The Dark One's moon is closest, playing havoc on coastal areas.

Brimgrog - Nuthaan's sacred brew. Few dare drink the burning brew, and of those few, most die. The rare Nuthaanians who survive the Rite are known (and feared) as Berserkers.

Brinehilde (brin·hillda) - A Nuthaanian Priestess of the Sylph who runs an orphanage in Drivel.

Carpinvale - A small fishing town in the south that exiled Oenghus.

Chaim (high·em) - A Guardian of Iilenshar, also known as the Guardian of Life and the River God. Son of Zahra, older brother to Asmara.

Circle of Nine - The ruling council of the Wise Ones.

Coven - A harbor town that sits directly beneath the stronghold of the Wise Ones.

Da'len - A barbarian tribe in Vaylin.

Dagenir (day·jen·near) - A Guardian of Morchaint, also known as the Dark One. He tried to steal the Orb, and battled with Zahra. The Orb shattered during their struggle.

Drivel - A large city on the Isle of Wise Ones.

Easthaven - The east side of the city of Haven, separated by the Gate and chasm.

Eiji (ee·Gee)- a gnome Wise One.

Ethervenom - An addicting drug made from harvested Plague Viper venom.

Everwar - The endless struggle between light and oblivion.

Fell Wastes - A harsh, mountainous region to the north of Nuthaan, populated by Wedamen.

Fey - Lindale (a race of elves) who rebelled against their nature and were twisted by their dark deeds.

Fomorri (fah·moor·ee) - A race created and twisted by the Fey's foul experiments.

Fyrsta (fears·tah) - The Sylph's favored realm.

Galvier Longstride - A legendary wanderer whose feet never stop moving.

Grawl - The Dark One's Own. Monstrous Voidspawn with void-like eyes.

Guardians of Iilenshar (ill·en·shar) - Six Guardians who survived the Shattering and were blessed with the Orb's power: Zahra, Chaim, Asmara, Zemoch, Oshimi, and Yvesa.

Guardians of Morchaint - Six Guardians who sided with the Void: Dagenir, Shade, Indrazor, Pazia, Mourn, and Silvanthe.

Gwaith - A Merchant kingdom along the Golden Road.

Haimon Goodfellow - Owner of the Glass Goblet.

Harsbane - A poisonous herb. The leaves contain an hallucinogen when smoked.

Hengist Heartfang - First Archlord of the Isle of Wise Ones.

Ielequithe (ill·ay·quith) - Lord General of the Isle of Wise Ones.

Iilenshar- Floating Isle of the Guardians. Coat of arms: the Sacred Sun caught in a maze-like circle.

Isiilde Jaal'Yasine (is·seal·dee jawl·yah·seen) - A combustible nymph with an affinity for fire.

Isek Beirnuckle - Spymaster to Marsais.

Isle of Blight - An island to the south of the Bastardlands that was ravaged when Ramashan, a druid, opened a Portal to the Nine Halls.

Isle of Winds - A grouping of islands off the Spotted Coast.

Isle of Wise Ones - An island off the Fell Coast where the Wise Ones Order is located.

Kambe (cam·bee) - A powerful kingdom ruled by Emperor Soataen Jaal III in the West.

Karbonek (car·bah·neck) - A Greater Fiend from the Nine Halls. A god revered by the Fomorri.

Keeper - A favored servant of the Sylph who was tasked with protecting Fyrsta.

Keening - The inhabitants of Fyrsta do not age like others. They only die of old age when the will to live fades. Someone who has lost the will to live is said to be in the Keening. As a result, many die in their twenties and thirties.

Kiln - A powerful kingdom to the East.

King's Folly - A game of runes that involves two hundred stones, and a cycle of ever-changing power.

Lindale - A race of elves (faerie) who were wiped out during the Shattering.

Lispen's Folly - A whirlpool of chaotic energy churning on the ceiling of the outer sanctum of the main hall, just outside of the Council Chambers of the Nine. Lispen was a Wise One who tried to open a Runic Portal, and disappeared.

Lome (low·meh) - A barbarian tribe in Vaylin.

Lucas Cutter - Paladin of the Blessed Order.

Luccub - An Imp with a tooth fetish.

Marsais (mar·say·es) - A sexy elf immortal.

Medwin - A barbarian tribe in Vaylin.

Miera Malzeen - A Wise One teacher who tried to link with Isiilde and was subsequently burned to a crisp.

Morigan Freyr (more·eh·gen fray·er) - Master Healer on the Isle of Wise Ones. Matriarch of the ruling Nuthaanian tribe. On and off Oathbound to Oenghus. Adopted mother of Isiilde. Savior of Nuthaan.

N'Jalss (nah·jaal·ss) - A Rahuatl Wise One.

Nereus (near·rose) - God of the seas.

Nine Halls - A realm that was overrun by the Void.

Oathbound - Inhabitants of Fyrsta take oaths, vowing to remain together as a couple for a specified amount of time determined by the couple.

Oenghus Saevaldr (oh·won·gus say·val·der) - A formidable Nuthaanian Berserker. Also known as: Wise One of the Isle, Bone Mender, Skull Crusher, the Bloody Berserker of Nuthaan and the Grimstorm of the Fell Wastes.

Oshimi (oh·shim·mee) - Guardian of Wisdom, also known as The Serene One.

Pip - A street urchin from the Dock Districts of Drivel. Brother to Zoshi and Tuck.

Pits o'Mourn - A deep chasm in Kiln. Criminals are lowered into the gorge and none ever emerge.

Pyrderi Har'Feydd (pie·deer·rhee haar·fade) - The first fey.

Rahuatl (raw·tule) - A race of humanoids who live in the Jungles of Rraal. Their culture is steeped in ritual and pain.

Rashk (rash·ka) - A Rahuatl Wise One who has a knack for enchanting.

Reapers - Voidspawn with a taste for fresh blood. Sometimes called Death's children.

Rivan (riv·en) - A young paladin of the Blessed Order.

Shattering - A powerful artifact that the Sylph imbued with her power to fight the Void. When Dagenir, its own guardian, attempted to steal the Orb for himself, Zahra tried to stop him. During their fight, the Orb was shattered, releasing a cataclysmic wave of power that nearly extinguished life on Fyrsta.

Shimei Al'eeth (shim·mee awl·eeth) - A Kilnish Wise One

Sidonie (sid·own·ee) - A Mearcentian Wise One

Soisskeli (soice·kill·ee) - The Chaos Lord who crafted a stave capable of opening Runic Gateways and binding any creature not of Fyrsta. Oshimi, the Serene One, defeated him in battle.

Somnial's Realm (salm·knee·el) - The Realm of Dreams, where all realms touch.

Spine - A tall, naturally formed spire that towers over the Wise Ones' stronghold.

Suevi (sweh·vee) - A barbarian tribe in Vaylin.

Sylph - The Goddess of All.

Tharios - A Wise One from Xaio.

Thedus - A sunburnt man who wanders around the Wise Ones' tower naked.

Thira Olander - Wise One of the Isle, Mistress of Novices, and High Alchemist.

Tuck - Urchin from the dock district in Drivel. Brothers: Pip and Zoshi.

Ulfhidhin (ulf·fid·hin) - The wild god who once abducted the Sylph and fought Karbonek.

Unspoken - or Disciples of Karbonek. A group of devout Bloodmagi who worship the Greater Fiend.

Void - Everything opposite of life.

Weeping Mark - A venomous spider.

Westhaven - The west side of the city of Haven, separated by the Gate and chasm.

Wisps - Tiny faeries who are often captured, put in jars, and used as a light source until they die.

Witchwood - A rare wood that has a natural resistance to enchantments.

Xiao (zow) - A merchant kingdom in the Bastardlands known for their pleasures.

Yvesa (yeh·veh·saa) - A Guardian of Iilenshar. A sprite who is revered by jesters and bards. She has a reputation for being a prankster.

Zahra (zah·rah) - A Guardian of Iilenshar, also known as the Radiant One, Goddess Of All That Was Just, Guardian of Good, and the Divine Savior. She battled with Dagenir when he tried to steal the Orb.

Zander - A Wise One who served Tharios, attacked Isiilde, and was burnt to a crisp.

Zianna (zee·anna) - A gifted Wise One's Apprentice.

Zoshi (zo·shee) - Urchin from Dock districts in Drivel. Brothers: Pip and Tuck.

CALENDAR OF FYRSTA

350 days in a year
10 Months in a year
35 days in a month

MONTHS

Wintertide
Thawing
Greentide
Sowing
Summertide
Faded
Harvest
Reddened
Carvers
Frostmarch

FESTIVALS

The Shadowed Dawn: 35th of Frostmarch to the 1st of Wintertide. Marks the new year with a night and a day of darkness, when all three moons align and the Dark One's own moon smothers the sun.

The Lightened Dusk: 17th-18th of Summertide. A day and a night of silver light when all three moons align and the Sylph's moon shines bright.

The Sylph's Fortnight: 10-24th Summertide. Fourteen days of Festivities dedicated to the Sylph.

Feast of Fools: 1-7th of Greentide. A week of costumed festivities that celebrate the end of winter.